PAMELA MARTIN

WAKING

the

DRAGON

RIVER GROVE
BOOKS

Published by River Grove Books
Austin, TX
www.rivergrovebooks.com

Distributed by River Grove Books

For ordering information or special discounts for bulk purchases, please contact River Grove Books at PO Box 91869, Austin, TX 78709, 512.891.6100.

Design and composition by Greenleaf Book Group LLC
Cover design by Greenleaf Book Group LLC
Cover images: (White House) ©iStockphoto.com/trekandshoot; (dragon) Tairy Greene, 2014. Used under license from Shutterstock.com.

Cataloging-in-Publication data
Martin, Pamela (Pamela M.)
  Waking the dragon / Pamela Martin.—First edition.

     pages ; cm.—([Hard whispers series] ; [book 2])

  Issued also as an ebook.

     1. Presidential candidates—United States—Fiction. 2. United States—Foreign relations—China. 3. China—Foreign relations—United States. 4. Adopted children—Fiction. 5. Presidents—China—Fiction. 6. Conspiracies—Fiction. 7. Suspense fiction. I. Title.

PS3613.A782 W35 2014
813/.6   2014935317

Print ISBN: 978-1-938416-77-4
eBook ISBN: 978-1-938416-78-1

First Edition

CHAPTER 1

São Paulo, Brazil
October 2009

As Marisol Vega darted across Rua Haddock Lobo, she caught sight of the massive fig tree that towered above Figueira Rubaiyat. The restaurant was one of the few places in Brazil where she felt safe. Marisol cursed the knee-length skirt she had worn that day. Thanks to it, she moved at more of a shuffle than a full run, but at least she'd had the sense to wear flats. From across the street, an elderly man standing behind a black wrought-iron gate looked on curiously at the sight of a fortysomething woman running full speed down the sidewalk glancing behind her every few seconds.

Marisol maintained her encumbered jog even as the rough-bricked pavement transitioned into jagged cement that pounded her feet. She felt certain her feet were bleeding by now, but she couldn't stop to check them—not until she was in the relative safety of the restaurant.

As she ran down the sidewalk, she noticed that Rua Haddock Lobo looked different somehow, like a nightmare version of her favorite spot. She had been down this street many times before, but she'd always seen it from the plush backseat of the limousine that carried her and her associates around the city.

How things have changed, she thought. *If only I'd never accepted that damn—*

She cut herself off. She had always been a staunch opponent of dwelling on *if*'s.

Figueira Rubaiyat was the best location she'd been able to think of at the time. It always had a steady crowd but was still off the beaten path. She just needed somewhere she could go to think and regroup—perhaps even make a phone call and explain her way out of it. Little hope rested in that option, but at least she would be in a familiar place, around people she knew.

She neared the restaurant, and the smell of grilled meat filled the humid air. She was close now, very close. The sight of the diners enjoying their meals on the other side of the freestanding glass wall outside the restaurant eased her tension a bit. The normalcy of the scene pulled her away, just for a moment, from the terribly surreal situation she now found herself in.

The façade of her normal existence had crumbled just a day before, in the moment she'd stood up from the conference table and announced that, though she was very honored to be considered a member of the group, it just wasn't for her. The faces staring back at her didn't convey disappointment; the women looked more like they were about to watch Marisol walk to the death chamber. Except, that is, for the their leader. She avoided eye contact with Marisol entirely, waiting silently for her to leave the room. Before Marisol even reached the door, the leader resumed the meeting as if nothing had happened.

When Marisol checked out of her hotel that evening, she noticed a man in the lobby who seemed to be watching her. She saw the same face at a local travel agent's office, then again at a coffee shop a few hours later. *Surely the rumors couldn't be true*, she had thought. But now she was certain she was being followed. She had to wonder, *Are they just monitoring me, or am I being tracked down like prey?*

The smart thing to do, she decided, was to err on the side of caution. If the man was simply keeping tabs on her, there was little she could do about that. But if she was a possible mark, she wasn't about to make it easy for him. She figured her best bet was to hide right out in the open.

Just as Marisol trotted up to the entrance of Figueira Rubaiyat, Renan Santoro—the restaurant's owner—stepped out of the black Mercedes he'd parked in front of the building. As he slammed the door behind him, he flashed Marisol his movie-star smile. "Ms. Vega! A most pleasant surprise!

Forgive me—I had no idea you and your friends were here tonight." He took her hand and bowed slightly to give it a light kiss.

Marisol did a quick check of the street behind her, and turned back to Renan. "I'm not with them this time, Rene. I'm alone and . . ." Marisol looked around again, and Renan did the same.

"Are you okay?" he asked. "Is someone following you?"

She considered pretending that everything was fine, but there was something about Renan that calmed her and made her feel comfortable. He had always been a good listener; they'd struck up a friendship after many long, wine-filled nights at his restaurant. She longed to tell him her story and be reassured that she was only being paranoid.

"I don't know, Rene. Something's happened and I . . ."

"I'll tell you what—come inside and let's sit down." He placed a gentle hand on her arm. "You look pale. Please take a rest. Today is on the house."

He guided her inside the restaurant and sat her at a table near the trunk of the enormous fig tree that had been beautifully incorporated into the architecture of the building.

"Order anything you want, Ms. Vega. I must check on the kitchen, but I'll be back in five minutes' time."

By the time Renan had returned, Marisol was on her second glass of chardonnay. She explained all her suspicions about the group of women that she accompanied to his restaurant several times a year. She told him about leaving the group and why she'd done it—and about the mysterious figure who seemed to be tailing her.

Once she finished, the color had drained from Renan's face. He sat, silent, with a wide-eyed look of shock. He seemed to have taken the story very seriously, and his concern only increased her own.

"My God, Ms. Vega. I wish you would've told me this before. I am so sorry . . . I had no idea."

Marisol patted Renan's hand. "Oh, come on now, it's okay. How could you have known? If I didn't know firsthand, I'd hardly believe it myself. To you, I'm sure we just looked like a group of old women spending up our retirement money. I didn't even—"

There was a loud shattering sound, and Renan and Marisol snapped their heads around. A blushing waitress crouched down to pick up the pieces of the plate she'd dropped. Even after realizing there was no need for alarm, Renan sat stiffly, a grave look frozen on his face.

"Relax, Rene. You're worse than me. Plus, I don't even think they'd actually—"

"No—listen, Ms. Vega. If this is all true, we have to get you—"

At that instant, the glass wall that shielded the outdoor seating shattered. The deafening sound of a rapid-firing weapon almost drowned out the high-pitched screams.

A man wearing dark sunglasses and a dark tailored suit rushed in from the main entrance.

Spotting Marisol immediately, he rushed to the table where she stood; she was too shocked to move. Renan watched, helpless, as the man pressed the muzzle of his gun against Ms. Vega's temple.

CHAPTER 2

Dallas, Texas
July 2012

Pamela Graham warily entered the mailroom on the bottom floor of her high-rise. She checked her mail here almost every day, usually choosing the evening hours in order to avoid the post-work mailroom rush. Tonight, something felt different. It was like she was being watched. The sensation was by no means new to her; just like the Texas heat, it's something no one ever gets truly accustomed to. Pam inserted her key into the tiny door of her mailbox and retrieved several letters. She flipped through the envelopes, searching for anything important. Besides a routine per-diem deposit receipt from her employer and a mysterious wax-sealed envelope, it was all bills and advertisements.

Just as she was about to turn around, she heard the mailroom door creak open behind her.

Damn it, thought Pamela. *Mrs. Childs strikes again.*

The front door of Esther Childs's apartment stood just feet from the mailroom. Mrs. Childs was the Bonaventure's oldest and most inquisitive resident, and she had a clear view of the mailroom from behind the blinds of her large picture window. Nearly every time she spotted a hapless mail-checker, Mrs. Childs popped out for a little chat that invariably turned into an extended conversation full of gossip presented as earth-shattering information. Pamela's energy was completely depleted from a day at work; she certainly didn't have the energy to do anything but collapse onto her couch. A talk with Mrs. Childs was out of the question.

Pamela shifted the envelopes in her hand for as long as she could, her body tensing as she waited for the shrieking singsong of Mrs. Childs's voice. She cut her eyes to the side. *That's odd. Surely Mrs. Childs would've said something by now.* There was no sound of the fumbling keys, no scuffle of flip-flops along the floor. No high-pitched voice screeching *"Hiii Pamela! I didn't know that was you!"*

Pam took a deep breath, then spun around just in time to see the door swinging back closed. The mailroom was empty. Whoever had come in hadn't checked a mailbox; the only sound Pam had heard was the person's entry. Her sensible side sorted through the possibilities: *Could have been security peeking in, or someone entering and realizing they forgot their keys.*

Pamela left the mailroom, looking up and down the sidewalk that ran along the high-rise, the entire area like a ghost town. The only movement came from the flashes of lightning in the distance, and the only sound from the soft thunder that followed. Inside the lobby, both the security guard and the newly hired concierge were missing.

Pam continued to the elevator, stepped inside, and pressed the button for the tenth floor. With a soft chime, the doors began to slowly slide together. Before her view of the lobby was completely cut off, she saw a man walking purposefully toward her. Pamela immediately froze and held her breath. *Please close. Please close.* The man met her eyes, quickly looked away, and then diverted his path from the elevator. Pamela exhaled gratefully as the doors closed, leaving her alone inside the elevator. As the elevator came to life, she lightly tapped the envelopes against her head. *Why am I so damn paranoid today?*

She flipped through the envelopes again as the elevator rose. Alex never let a week go by without sending something. But still nothing from him today—just that strange wax-sealed letter. *Probably some fancy junk mail,* she thought.

Once inside her apartment, Pamela kicked off her heels in the small entry and made a left down the hall, tossing her mail onto the dining table. She passed into the living room, clicked on the television, and pulled open the blinds. As the familiar voices of world-news reporters chattered on behind her, she gazed out her balcony window at the lightning darting across the horizon behind the Dallas skyline. Despite the beauty of the view, she couldn't stop dwelling on the feeling that someone was out to get her.

She made a quick trip to the kitchen, poured herself a glass of pinot noir, and then resumed her place at the window, getting lost in the towering buildings and the turbulent, darkening sky. She sipped the wine, trying not to think about the mailroom or the man in the lobby.

A flash of light illuminated the top of a parking garage several floors below her apartment. In the split second of light, Pam spotted a person standing at the top of the garage. It seemed to be a man, and he held a pair of binoculars that pointed straight at her apartment.

CHAPTER 3

Pamela's heart raced as she looked down at the watcher through the sliding glass doors. Without the lightning, she could only make out a vague outline. She tried to unearth a rational explanation, desperate to put aside the thought that she was being watched. Her intuition wouldn't let her. She knew they were watching her.

It was the first time in nearly a decade that someone had been this aggressive in monitoring her. In the years since her brief but deadly entanglement with the CIA, she had often felt that people were tailing her, keeping tabs on her. At first she had felt despair; she was a caged woman in a free world. There were shifty glances from alleyways; the ever-present clicking noises during phone calls; cars that seemed to always take the same route as her. As time passed, she waited for the surveillance to taper off. Surely they would stop observing her at some point. Now, peering through the dark at this man, a bitter but familiar taste spread across her palate.

Pamela folded her arms and swished the wine around in her glass, affecting a cool, confident stance. Another flash—the man was still brazenly staring right at her through the binoculars. He must have noticed that she was looking back by now, but he was apparently unfazed. The longer she saw his outline against the dark grays of the parking garage, the more real the situation became.

Behind her, urgent drumbeats and a sober baritone voice from the television announced a breaking news item. "We interrupt regularly scheduled programming to bring you this special report." The newscaster's words filled her living room, and she wished she could turn from the balcony, forget the man, and enjoy an hour or two of CNN.

Pamela narrowed her eyes even tighter and felt her forehead tighten. She scowled as rising anger began to dominate her fear. The binoculars were aimed directly at her through the sliding glass doors, invading her privacy—her home. At last the stranger lowered his binoculars, but he continued to look straight toward her balcony. Pam wasn't about to back down; she scowled stubbornly at the shadowy figure, digging her toes into the thick white carpet. She wouldn't be the first to look away. *What in the hell are you looking at?*

The man raised the binoculars back to his face. Pamela's first inclination was to take the elevator down to the first floor and sprint across the street to confront the stranger. But what good would that do? It wasn't as if the stranger would hang out and wait for her as she ran up to him.

Besides, even if she were able to catch him, what good would it do? The English-accented words of her friend Giles came to mind: *"Individuals—most of the time, anyway—are just the eyes of a bigger organization."*

That was exactly what worried her. Suppressing the impulse to close the blinds and put the whole thing out of her mind, she stared back at the faceless stranger. There was no chance she could get a clear view of the man's face; it was too dark, and he was too far away. So she picked up what details she could—the slender build, the black clothes, the casual body language, the self-assured posture.

Could this just be some creep? A Peeping Tom? There it was—the futile second-guessing. She had tried to get past that, put faith in her own intuition. It had gotten her out of Russia and helped her foil powerful enemies all those years ago. She couldn't push it aside now and hope for blissful ignorance. Soft thunder rumbled in the far distance. As more dark clouds collected over the city, Pamela thought about all the dark corners her watcher would be able to hide in.

Pamela flinched when the doorbell sounded. She immediately admonished herself. *The doorbell shouldn't have that effect on you, Pamela. This is your home.* She turned back to the view from her balcony, but her observer was gone. Pamela scanned the street inch by inch, desperately trying to spot him again. He had vanished.

Hesitantly, she moved from the balcony and made her way to the front door. Irrational thoughts filled her head: *Are they here for me? Why did they wait so long? Get a grip, Pam. Get a grip.*

She picked up the silver letter opener from the dining table and teetered on the edge of a full panic attack. About ten feet away, the hallway made a right angle and became the front entry; when she had moved into the condo seven years before, she'd hated not being able to see the front door from down the hall.

The doorbell had been silent since the first ring. *Calm down, Pamela. You're overreacting.*

She stopped in her tracks when she heard a click. The sound of a twisting doorknob was unmistakable. *Did I leave it unlocked?*

Click. Click. It sounded like someone had opened the door and then closed it again quickly. She stood, paralyzed, just out of sight of the entry.

Her throat constricted, and the sound of her swallow was deafening in the hushed hallway. The three-inch blade of the letter opener quivered in her petrified hand.

If she ran to her bedroom, she could get the gun tucked inside the Manolo shoebox under her bed. It had saved her life once before.

Ding-dong! Ding-dong!

Pam inhaled sharply and let out a tiny shriek as the doorbell chimed again. There was another click, and a block of light fell onto the wall of the hallway from the corridor outside, darkened by the outline of a person. The shadow disappeared as the door closed. The tongue of the doorknob clicked back into place.

Someone was standing in the entry.

CHAPTER 4

Pamela backed down the hall, the letter opener extended in front of her like a miniature sword. Her palms were moistened, her breathing rapid. Spinning around in a smooth, catlike motion, she made a break for the bedroom. *The gun. I have to get the gun.*

"Pam!"

At the sound of her best friend's voice, Pamela abandoned her sprint and spun back around. She turned to see Roxy standing in the hallway with a bemused smirk on her collagen-enhanced lips. Pam blew out a long, relieved breath.

"What on earth are you doing, girl?" her friend asked.

"Roxy! You scared the hell out of me!"

Roxy eyed Pamela up and down. "Did I?"

Pamela leaned forward with one hand over her chest, still fighting to catch her breath. "Hell, Rox . . ."

"A li'l jumpy, aren't we?" Roxy's half-smile faded when she saw how frightened Pam really was. She placed a manicured hand on her friend's arm. "Wait a sec—sorry, Pam . . . I really didn't mean to scare you."

Pam went to the door and poked her head out as Roxy walked toward the living room. She had no idea why her front door was unlocked. She never failed to secure it—and check the lock several times. She dead-bolted the door and returned to the living room. Roxy was rapidly flipping through the channels on the television, giving each less than two seconds of a chance.

"Rox, change that back for me. I was kind of watching something."

Roxy sat slumped on the couch with her back to Pam. "What? The news? I don't know how you find that interesting. It's the same crap every day. So and so's up in the polls. Gas prices are up this much. We owe the Chinese that much. All the time!"

"Just switch it back. You'll have to catch *Entertainment Tonight* or whatever it is you want to watch in the other room."

Roxy sighed. "Whatever you say." With a sympathetic smile, she gave Pam the remote and patted her hand. "I'll skip the tube for now, sweetie. I need to freshen up a bit anyway. It's too damn humid out there. I think I need to move to a drier climate. Texas is killing my hair." Roxy disappeared around the corner and into the bathroom.

Pam switched the television back to CNN; it was on a commercial break. She walked back over to the balcony door and looked down. The watcher was still gone.

Roxy continued the conversation from the bathroom. "So how's the love life?" she yelled.

"Love life? Where'd that come from?" Pam shouted back.

"What?"

"Why are you asking about my love life?" Pam said, her irritation growing.

"Oh, it's like that now? Does Pammy have a secret?"

"What the hell are you talking about?"

"What?" Roxy shouted.

"Never mind!" Pam turned up the volume on the television, hoping to drown out her friend's drawl.

"So what's his name?" Roxy said from the bathroom, still attempting to keep up the conversation. "Is this a new guy?"

"First of all, Rox, I'm trying to watch the news. Second, I have no idea what the *hell* you're talking about."

"I'm talking about that guy! The one leaving when I came up."

Pam lowered the volume on the TV and stood from the couch. "Leaving my place? Tonight?"

"Duh! The guy walking out of your apartment when I walked up!"

CHAPTER 5

The Republican primaries for the 2012 presidential ticket had begun as a mudslinging contest overflowing with scandalous accusations. Millions of Americans had sat captivated in front of their televisions, watching the results on that Super Tuesday months earlier. One man had been cutthroat enough to come out ahead of the pack, a man who embodied everything the Democrats feared. He had already lit a fire under a massive following, and his group of vociferous backers continued to grow every day. His campaign had started out as a late-night–talk-show punch line, but somehow it had grown into something very real.

Apprehension about the Republican candidate stretched beyond the opposing party. Among those closely watching the election were many businessmen and foreign officials on the opposite side of the globe, each of whom had a vested interest in this particular man *not* moving up the political ladder. Bankers, businessmen, and government dignitaries all across China were collectively glued to their television sets.

As for most of the Chinese middle class, they had little to no interest in the election. Most of China's population lived a lifestyle that most Americans would never achieve. In the midst of a booming economy, employers were finding it harder and harder to attract workers of any kind. The lower classes were slowly disappearing, being consumed into the burgeoning middle class.

For the top 5 percent of the wealthy in the People's Republic of China, the outcome meant far more than a routine change in government leaders. The result of the election could send shockwaves across the Pacific Ocean, altering life as they knew it.

* * *

Inside the walls of one of the most exclusive office towers in China, Li Bin watched as his father, President Yang Bin, stared at the sixty-inch flat-screen television that hung on the bright red wall. The president sat at the edge of a massive mahogany chair trimmed with fourteen-karat gold, flanked by two government officials and his personal assistant. The old man leaned forward, his spine deeply curved. Li could see his father's bloodshot eyes and hear his quick, agitated breathing.

This was not supposed to happen, and it's killing my father.

President Bin remained stone faced as a headshot of the man he had grown to despise appeared on the high-definition screen. There before him was the face of Republican candidate Donald Wynn, right next to new poll numbers. For the first time, Wynn was polling ahead of the Democratic president in popularity and on economic issues.

Like his father, Li knew all about this man, and nothing he knew pleased him. Word of Wynn's vitriolic condemnation of China had quickly crossed the Pacific. The candidate's rants against Li's homeland had become legendary. He could tell the mere sight of the man raised his father's blood pressure.

Several times, President Yang Bin opened his mouth in preparation to speak, but each time he stopped himself. Li glanced at the two officials sitting to the left of his father, assessing how they were handling the situation. *Not now, Father, not now.*

President Bin wrung his hands. It was now clear to everyone in the room that what they'd prayed would not occur was now happening. Wynn was far from a joke now. He was a real contender, and with these poll numbers, he was one giant step closer to the presidency. Yang Bin turned toward his son and shook his head gravely.

The television switched to footage of a Wynn rally. Wynn gripped the surface of the podium with each hand and leaned to the microphone. Before he could say a word, another roar erupted from the sea of supporters. Wynn appeared to be soaking in the adoration, feeling the love as he scanned the vast assembly of supporters.

"I hear you loud and clear!" Wynn began. "It's just an early poll, but I'll tell you what." He shoved a finger at the crowd to accent each word. "We have a lot of people shaking—in—their—boots!" The crowd howled with approval.

President Bin wrung his hands even harder. "Damn him!" he shouted. Li was startled by this break in his father's typically controlled demeanor. Now that he was so close to winning the White House, Wynn apparently had no intentions of giving up his pet cause. If anything, he was hammering his signature issue in even harder.

The message seemed to appeal to most Americans. According to his speeches, Wynn was committed to making China pay for the policies that had allowed them to take advantage of America. Should he win the presidency, he was committed to placing heavy tariffs on every single one of China's imports. He felt it was his duty to alert the American people— Republican and Democrat—to their common enemy on the other side of the world.

"I can assure you that taxing China is the single most important thing we can do to get our country out of debt," Wynn had shouted again and again on the campaign trail. "It's the only way we can get out from under their wing, and create more jobs on our own soil."

Although his father had been wary of Wynn from the beginning, Li considered the man loud but harmless. That sentiment changed as Wynn's bid for the most powerful office in the world became the top international news story. Li now considered him dangerous and unpredictable, and he followed his father's orders to monitor Wynn's progress twenty-four hours a day.

"He is always making moves now for the future," President Bin had said. "A very dangerous man, son." Li had to admit that the campaign had been an astounding success.

The reality was that a US president had lost a race for a second term only three times in the entire history of the country, but Wynn had raised hundreds of millions in record time and was ready to put up the long-odds fight. He'd even done some extensive research and made the decision to switch parties three years before the campaign. That way, he could face the current regime head on, dramatically strengthening his odds. Once he won the Republican ticket, he had been able to collectively bring about other anti-Democratic parties to join him.

President Bin's eyes darted to the screen as he gripped the arms of the chair. Li felt helpless as he watched his suffering father. The situation only heightened his disdain for the American presidential candidate.

Only one happy thought kept Li from being totally absorbed by his family's concerns. The next day he was headed to Spain for a long-planned adventure with his best friend and former roommate at Brown. He hoped things would settle down a bit before he returned home. If not, something would need to be done—would *have* to be done.

CHAPTER 6

Roxy hummed to herself as she teased her dark brown curls with a tiny pink comb. Pam couldn't help but marvel at the trancelike focus Roxy always had in front of the mirror. When Roxy turned and saw Pam in the doorway, she stopped toying with her hair. "Damn, what's up with the serious look? You all right?"

"Rox, who did you see leaving my apartment?"

Roxy held up her hands in mock surrender. "No big deal, girl. I don't even know who he was. You don't have to worry about me spreading your business around." Roxy winked as she turned back to her own reflection.

"No—Rox, honey, listen. I didn't have anyone here. I think the guy you saw was trying to break in."

This finally caught Roxy's full attention. "What? I don't think so. He seemed way too calm, and normal looking." Roxy tapped the comb against her chin in thought. "I mean, he did seem a little surprised, but I just thought I'd startled him. I was going to say something to him but he looked away and walked on down the hall. I assumed you guys were trying to keep your little tryst under wraps."

"Oh my God. What did he look like?"

"Medium height, stocky, jet-black hair . . . five o'clock shadow . . ."

Pam's eyebrows pulled together in a frown. "That's so strange."

"I know. And since it looked like he'd just closed the door, I just walked right in."

The color had drained from Pamela's face. "This isn't good."

Roxy's mouth fell slowly open in a delayed realization. "You don't think that . . ."

"What?"

"I mean, you don't think someone is still after you, do you?"

Pam shook her head. "I don't know. One day I'm thinking it's just my imagination and the next day I'm convinced they never stopped trying to get me. Just before you got here, I saw a guy downstairs looking at me . . . oh God." Pam massaged her forehead with her fingertips. "I just can't go through all this again."

"I know, hon. I know we didn't talk about it much, but you went through a lot back then. Those Russian police guys came after you for taking Alex out of the orphanage. And then—it still sounds so crazy today—that whole vaccine thing. They were going to wipe out half the country! You had the CIA after you—gunfights, secret documents, near-death experiences and all."

Pamela forced a weak smile. It was still hard to believe that she'd helped foil a government plot to wipe out millions of innocent Americans with a tainted vaccine in a cold-blooded scheme to boost the economy. After she'd gotten the damning information to her friend Giles—a man with the means to blast it across the Internet—the government had done a brilliant cleanup job, shoving blame on Joseph, the very man who'd done so much to prevent the catastrophe. "I don't know, Rox. I hardly think about that stuff anymore. It was so long ago."

"Uh-huh. You can play Braveheart if you want, but that was hell. In my book, you have every right to be a little keyed up now and then. And I mean . . . couldn't they still be after you for knowing way too much?"

"I'm pretty sure they're not."

"What makes you think that?" Roxy asked.

"Mainly the fact that I'm still alive."

* * *

An hour later, Pam sat in the living room, absently scanning the snow-white carpet for discolorations. The television was muted for the commercial break in the newscast. She could hear Roxy, now dawdling in Pam's bedroom, as she hummed the verse of "Hotel California" over and over.

Pam stood and peered out the balcony doors. She was struggling to keep her mind off the man at her door and the man with the binoculars. The doorbell had rung while she was watching the man down below; that meant there was more than one of them. She pressed mute as the evening news returned from the commercial break. *"In other news, the Dow Jones Industrial Average has dropped for the twenty-third consecutive day."*

Roxy called out to Pam from the bedroom. "Oh my gosh, the guy who wrote this book is a *stud!*"

"What book?" Pam shouted without taking her eyes from the screen.

"The one on your nightstand! *Ninety-Three Percent Says It All.*"

"He is a handsome man, Rox. But that's about all I think you'd like about it." In the nearly fifteen years Pam had known Roxy, she'd never seen her with a book.

Roxy walked in from the bedroom, the paperback in her hand. "What's it about?"

"Body language. The author talks about how ninety-three percent of communication is nonverbal. I took a few classes on reading body language and got that book to brush up. It's pretty good if you're interested in the subject."

"Nah. But this author could show me his body language anytime." Roxy plopped down onto the couch.

CHAPTER 7

Wynn had worked up a sweat as he rallied the crowd, shouting and gesticulating wildly. The latest poll numbers had come in, and the good news had sent the assembled crowd into a roar that lasted for five long minutes.

"I know I have some people scared out there," Wynn shouted into the microphone. "And it's not just my opponent. Everyone knows that when I am elected president my first agenda will be to put an end to China's manipulation of our currency. We're gonna place a tariff on every towel, toy, and toothpick that comes into our country!"

The eruption was so loud that television crews scrambled to lower the volumes on their headsets. Wynn tried to get in another sentence, but the din of the crowd was too much to overcome. He bellowed into the microphone anyway, hammering his fist against the wooden podium. "It is time to pay the piper, and I guarantee you that China will feel my wrath!"

The audience danced around with their flags and banners, drowning out most of his words. They were sold, no matter what he was saying.

Once the cheering subsided slightly, Wynn's raspy voice lashed out at President Bin's government again. "Hey, listen . . . Listen!" Wynn extended his arms, palms outward. "I don't know about my opponent, but I love this country. And you all know that I'm not one to sugarcoat my words. Once

I'm in office, you can bet every casino chip in the world that I will put a stop to China's fleecing of the United States of America!"

The crowd loved it.

"Look. I know these guys. I've worked with these guys. I've sold real estate to these guys. They think we're idiots! They're laughing at us while they charge us the highest interest rates in the world and loan it back to us. Well, China, it's last call. That—party—is—*over*!"

Wynn had brought the crowd to an absolute frenzy. Signs and banners waved above the crowd, displaying brightly colored messages: "Wynn for President," "The Real Wynn Card," "China, you're fired!" Decks of playing cards with Wynn's image were tossed into the air along with confetti. Clusters of red, white, and blue balloons rose into the air.

 Wynn stretched his hands outward and fanned them down in a lost effort to quiet the crowd. "Listen—hold on a sec. Listen!"

The noise decreased slightly.

"This isn't just talk. I have a plan. When I get into office, I intend to slap China with a twenty-five percent tax on *all* of that low-quality crap they ship over here. And I'll use that revenue to pay off the bulk of the over trillion dollars of debt that they hold over our heads! We don't need their junk. We need to buy American products. We need to put Americans to work!"

* * *

"Enough!"

President Yang Bin swung his arm wildly, knocking over the stand next to his chair. The priceless Ming dynasty tea set donated to the Bin family by a local antique shop lay shattered across the tiled Pietra Firma floor. Li Bin quickly muted the television and nodded at his father's assistant, who rushed over to sweep up the broken porcelain.

His father looked haggard as he rose from his seat. As far as Li knew, he hadn't eaten a full meal in days. His father's hand shook with fury as he tried to get the words out.

"He . . . he will be a problem!"

Like many others, Li worried that the pressure was affecting his father's health. Stress had already become a daily fixture in Li's life. After the insistence of his father, he'd taken over the operation of Sinopec, his father's most successful company, and the constant pressure of overseeing daily operations was beginning to take its toll. The previous week, his doctor has prescribed him pills to keep his blood pressure down. Meanwhile, businesses controlled by the Bin family grew by the month. The multibillion-dollar oil companies controlled by his family had recently opened large operations in Canada and South America, ever in search of more global expansion.

Li missed life as a student studying abroad in America. He smiled as he remembered those days. Against his father's wishes, he still managed to remain in contact with a few of his American friends—one in particular, a guy he'd befriended in Spain. If his father knew what Li planned to do on his trip, he'd lose his mind.

Li's flight was set to leave that very night, and his bags had been packed for weeks. Spain wasn't America, but he couldn't wait for a short break from his father's unending struggle for more power and the strain of leading Sinopec.

If he had a choice, he would happily pass on his position as CEO of Sinopec, return to America, and continue his education. But that wasn't going to happen. According to his father, school was no longer important.

"Graduate school?" President Bin would tell his son. "Four years is enough. Now you learn in the real world."

Despite his frustration, Li did realize the importance of working at Sinopec. Family wasn't a topic he took lightly; it was the way of the Chinese affluent after all. President Bin and his close friends lobbied top US companies like JP Morgan and Goldman Sachs to hire their children in order to feed their business strategies. These Chinese bankers and businessmen frequently had prestigious Western college degrees obtained after the Cultural Revolution, a decade or two of experience, and a deep understanding of what Wall Street needed to succeed in China. The ballooning business prompted big US and multinational firms to fill out their operations with a younger cadre of China's elite. Many of the newer hires were referred to as princelings because they descended from well-connected families, if not Communist Party leaders.

"Transition of leadership has come," his father often said. "We will be the generation that will take the vision of the ones who came before us to establish a wiser, younger regime. Soft power is the answer."

Exactly what that "soft power" meant, Li had always been afraid to ask. Sinopec, under his father's guidance, made a lot of moves that Li did not understand. When President Bin insisted that the board of directors approve the acquisition of a Canadian oil-exploration company for $7.2 billion, Li was furious. He'd been pushing to purchase a less expensive, more productive company right there in China, but his father quickly shot down his plan.

That day, Li had been tempted to step down, going so far as to confront his father. "I just don't get this constant drive for overseas expansion. It doesn't make any sense to me," Li said after pleading his case.

His father remained stone faced, unmoved by the plea. After a few moments, President Bin placed an uncharacteristically consoling hand on Li's shoulder.

"Not every war is fought with weapons, son," he said. "And although they do not realize it yet, flowing water wears away rock. Make no mistake: We are at war, and we are already winning."

CHAPTER 8

It pained Li to see his aging father so wholly consumed by an election that was taking place on the other side of the world. Some days, he questioned his father's mental stability. Part of Li understood the importance of the election, but would it really matter that much in the long run? Wynn would make things hard on China for a while if he won the presidency, but surely the obstacle could be overcome.

Li had expressed this line of reasoning to his father a few weeks before. "This man can say whatever he wants, Father, but even if he wins, it would take a lot of time and effort to do everything he claims he will. He'd need two full terms to carry it all out. And I can't imagine the American people would go along with a lot of it."

President Bin hadn't looked at his son when he responded. "It is up to the farmer to pick which plants are allowed to grow. Some should be supported, and others should never be allowed to sprout."

After that conversation, Li decided to permanently drop the subject. At twenty years old, he was conditioned to give in to things he didn't quite understand, even if solely for the sake of the family. His days at Brown—a time when he was free to disagree with anyone around him—seemed a hopeless vision. Had any of his schoolmates gone back to fathers like this? Li doubted it.

He compared his life to that of his best friend's, the one who now lived in Spain. His friend's e-mails were dominated by the common theme of happiness. He wrote about the joy of pursuing the goals he had set years ago when they were still college roommates. Li found himself jealous of the choices his friend had been allowed to make. In China, tradition was not optional.

A hard cough from President Bin interrupted Li's daydream. The assistant rushed over with a glass of water, but the old man waved it off. When Li's father began coughing again, Li placed a hand on his back. He could feel the rattle inside the chest cavity. The two government officials looked on uneasily.

"Father, I don't think we need to get too troubled over this." Li tried to lead his father back to his chair, but the president pulled away. "He's only been nominated by the Republicans. He still has to win the election before we get really concerned."

President Bin slowly walked over to the floor-to-ceiling window that served as the west wall of his office and gazed out of the smoked glass. He remained stiff, hands clasped behind his back, silently watching the cars pass along bustling Haidian Zhichun Road. In the sunlight that beamed through the glass, Li couldn't help noticing the deepened wrinkles of his father's face.

President Bin started to speak but paused. He turned to the assistant and the two government officials and gestured toward the door. All three men marched out of the room without words. Only Li and his father remained in the lavishly furnished office.

"I see that you don't fully understand, my son. We cannot afford to wait for this man to gain power and then react. One does not wait for a falling object to touch his head before he tries to move from under it."

Li lowered his head. "Yes, Father." It was rare that he so quickly grasped one of his father's analogies.

President Bin placed his trembling hands on his son's shoulders.

"So much to learn. One day I will need you to continue the traditions my ancestors and I have set in place. It is up to us to continue them. Our grip must remain firm, but achieved through soft power."

"Yes, Father. I understand." *Sort of.*

The president looked back to the still-muted television. Donald Wynn stood in the center of the stage surrounded by his family, all waving at the rally crowd.

President Bin moved closer to the television, hands clasped behind his back. He spoke again with his eyes locked on the silent screen.

"It is said that a crisis is an opportunity riding in dangerous wind." He turned to Li. "So I hear that you have travels tomorrow?"

"Yes sir. Spain."

"Ah yes, Spain. A most beautiful country. You are meeting investors in Madrid, correct?"

"Yes sir," Li lied.

"So, Zhao Xin will travel with you."

Li had expected this response from his father and already had a solution in place. His father always insisted that he travel with their female bodyguard—she was five foot ten and built like a linebacker. But the last thing Li needed on this trip was an extra pair of eyes and the risk of word getting back to his father. This trip would have to be done solo.

President Bin tore himself from the television and crossed the tiled floor in short, purposeful steps.

Li cleared his throat. "No sir, Zhao will not be with me on this trip."

President Bin looked up. "Yes, she will. It is required."

"Yes sir, I know, but she too is traveling now," Li replied.

President Bin stared at his son, waiting for further explanation. Li cleared his throat and pointed to the television. "I had her travel to the United States, sir, to keep a closer watch on the candidate."

President Bin gave him a barely perceptible nod. "This is good. Zhao is the best person we could have to keep an eye on *that* man." President Bin sneered at the image of Wynn on the television.

Li let out a breath of relief.

President Bin now stood by a stand that held a tiny bonsai tree planted in a small oak box. He peered down at the tree, leaning in to scrutinize every inch.

"Looks like I have been neglecting my duties," he said, pointing to the tiny branches. The bonsai tree had not been attended to in weeks, and a single miniature branch protruded from the undersized leaves. President

Bin twisted the branch between his wrinkled fingers. "The bonsai is not a demanding tree. See here? If it were not for this one part sticking out, I may have not even noticed it was getting out of hand."

Removing a pair of tiny shears from a compartment in the stand, President Bin snipped off the small branch and tossed it roughly onto the polished floor.

CHAPTER 9

Pamplona, Spain

"The *encierro!*" a frantic voice wailed from deep within the crowd of anxious runners.

Alexander Dezcallar de Mazarredo felt his heart leap in his chest the instant the first rocket went off. The corral gates had been opened. On his immediate left, his best friend anxiously bounced up and down, his slender frame relaxed and ready.

Alex stood stiff, his wide eyes darting in every direction. His friend turned toward him with a confidant grin and held up five fingers. Alex nodded. *Yeah, I remember. The running of the bulls only lasts five minutes. But—*

When the second rocket went off, the swarm of runners bolted from the starting area, stumbling into one another as they dashed along the first portion of the nine-hundred-yard stretch. Alex tore ahead of the crowd, keeping an even pace with his friend. Many of the runners choked, breaking away and jumping off the course mere seconds after the race began.

The ground shook from the pounding hooves of the twelve bulls that stampeded through the narrow, jam-packed cobblestone streets of Pamplona. Alex maintained a steady stride as he glanced over at his friend Li, who was outpacing him. Li streaked in front of the other runners like a gazelle, a red scarf hanging from the belt of his white outfit.

As he ran from the agitated herd, Alex now wondered how Li had talked him into doing this. *At least I'm not wearing one of those damn scarves.*

The stampede felt like much more than just a dozen bulls. Alex imagined thousands of the powerful animals on his tail. Glancing to his left, Alex saw that Li had kept up his effortless nonchalance in the face of danger, but Alex felt like he was falling farther and farther behind. He could now hear the grunts of the massive beasts behind him. It felt like they were inches behind him, but he was too scared to look back. This was far more terrifying than he'd expected. Perspiration poured down his body, gluing his white cotton shirt to his back.

At last he cupped his hands over his mouth and shouted to his friend, doing his best to maintain a full run.

"Li! Li! I'm bailing!" He pointed to an opening in the wooden barrier just a few feet ahead of them and drifted to the far right.

"Punk!" Li yelled back, laughing. "Sorry you suck!"

That was all it took to convince Alex to drift back into the crowd of runners. He shot right past the opening he'd planned to slip through. Li raised both hands in triumph when he saw that his friend was still in.

"I'm staying!" Alex shouted above the din of the stampede and the screaming spectators. "Looks like it's *you* that sucks!"

Alex's decision gave him a renewed focus, but he was still losing ground to the beasts behind him. *Just five minutes. I can do this.*

Two minutes later, Alex had lost sight of Li, and he could feel the hot breath of the beasts shooting from their nostrils. Out of the corner of his eye, he saw one runner get brutally shoved into the crowd by the fastest bull.

Suddenly, Alex let out a loud grunt and realized his feet were no longer touching the ground.

One of the bulls had butted its massive head into Alex's back, tossing his body forward. Alex went airborne for longer than he thought was humanly possible, but somehow he managed to land on his feet in full stride. The bull's horns had extended on each side of Alex, missing his torso, but one horn had cut the inside of his right arm. Blood leaked from the gash and splattered across his all-white running outfit.

Alex's stride broke and he fell to the sidewalk as the other runners hurtled past in the cobblestone street. It felt like the muscles in his leg had snapped in half.

"Damn it!" he screamed in pain.

The impact of the fall had knocked the wind out of him, and he was virtually helpless as he felt a bull's horn impale his right leg. He howled in pain, his face pressed against the rough sidewalk.

Something impossibly heavy now crushed his other leg. He heard shouts and saw the feet of spectators rushing his way.

Everything went dark.

CHAPTER 10

Pamela sat in her dining room, sipping her second cup of coffee. Her unopened day planner lay next to her, ignored along with six new voice mails in her cell phone. Her green eyes, swollen and red from lack of sleep, gazed into the middle distance, unfocused.

The doorbell snapped her out of her daze. She set her coffee on its glass coaster, stood from the table, and cautiously made her way down the hall.

This time Pamela was prepared for anything. After Roxy's sighting of the stranger at her door, she'd relocated her handgun from the box under her bed to the wide-mouthed silver vase that stood in the hallway by the entry. As she'd weighed the weapon in her hands and placed it in its new home, dark memories stirred in her mind. A shot ringing out in the night. The agent's body, slumped in a dark alley behind a Spanish restaurant.

The doorbell sounded again. Someone rapped harshly against the door, then followed up with an angry twist of the doorknob and more chiming from the bell. The persistent style of the visitor actually caused Pam to relax. There was only one person it could be. Though she was now positive of who was on the other side of the door, she placed her eye to the peephole just to be sure.

A man with broad shoulders and silver hair stood outside, impatiently craning his neck to the right as if looking for another way inside.

Dad. What in the world are you doing here?

She slid the dead bolt open and opened the door.

"Well, well, well. You can answer the door!" her father said. "You sure as hell can't answer the phone." He marched right past her on his way inside.

"Hello to you too, Daddy," Pam said under her breath.

"What's going on with you? I've been trying to call you for the past two days. I thought that you never made it back from your work trip. Where'd Formula One send you this time, Afghanistan?"

Here we go. Pam pinched the bridge of her nose and placed a hand on her hip. "No, I was in Sweden. They don't have Formula One tracks in Afghanistan."

"Really? I'm sure that will change."

"I doubt it, Dad."

"So where to next?" he asked as he eyed the living room.

"Shanghai," she said.

Benjamin Graham raised his eyebrows. "Oh really? And you think that's any better than Afghanistan?" He turned and marched into the dining room. "Hey, is that coffee I smell? How about getting your dad a cup?"

"Sure, Dad. Black?"

"As always," he replied. As she stood at the coffeemaker and poured him a cup, she saw him pick up the tall green mug she'd been drinking from—a souvenir from her first trip to Spain. "Talked to Alexander lately?"

Pamela paused. The question was out of character for her father. They rarely talked about Alex, and when they did it was she who brought him up. "Yeah, I spoke to him last week. He's doing fine. He's supposed to visit again this summer."

Benjamin hitched up his pants at the knees and lowered himself into a chair at the dining table. "So I hear that they just hired him at Mazarredo. They're doing pretty well for themselves over there. Just inked a deal to purchase another oil company right there in Spain, and I hear they've got some other investments in the works. How old is that kid now?"

"He's twenty, about to turn twenty-one."

"I'll be damned. I bet he's made old Jorge one proud papa. Hell of a kid!"

Pam saw where this was going, but it was too late to change the subject.

"So Formula One is making you go to Shanghai?"

"They're not *making* me." She set down a steaming mug of coffee in front of her father and headed back to the coffeemaker to freshen her own up.

"So you don't have to go if you don't want to?"

She continued to humor him. "Of course not. I go because it's my job and I like what I do. Can we get through one conversation without you telling me how much I should hate working for Formula One?"

Benjamin shook his head. "You sound just like your mother sometimes."

"Is that supposed to be a bad thing?"

"It ain't good, that's for sure." Benjamin took a sip of coffee. "But don't get me wrong—your mom was a hell of a lady," he said in a lighter tone.

"I know, Dad. I still miss her. Next week makes twenty years since she's been gone."

Benjamin frowned. "Twenty years? You sure? I'll be damned."

The sight of the silver vase down the hallway gave Pam a thought. "Hey, Dad, can I ask you something? I've been having—"

Benjamin's phone rang and he quickly pulled it out of his jacket, holding up his index finger to quiet Pam.

"What? Who the hell told you that?" he barked into the phone. "Look, this clusterfu—this is falling apart, and till we get someone in there who's gonna do something, it ain't gonna get any better. Hell, I may have to ask for my campaign donation back just to keep us afloat! . . . Listen, I am at my daughter's place, but I'll be in the office later on to sort this out."

"Bad news, Daddy?" Pam said, leaning against the dining room table with her cup of coffee cradled in her hand.

Benjamin brushed a hand through his thinning silver hair. "You don't know the half of it. You been watching the news?"

"Of course, every day," Pam replied.

"Yeah, well they don't know half of it either! They prattle on about gas prices and the weak dollar, shi—I mean crap like that, instead of the real problem."

"And what's the *real* problem?"

"I can't tell you for sure, but something big is going on out there. There are too many things happening at the same time for it to be just a coincidence. Your grandfather used to say that if you keep falling on your ass in a crowd of people, you might want to take a closer look at everyone around you—more than likely, someone's tripping you."

Between sips of coffee, Pam tried to figure out what her father was getting at. He was being pretty ambiguous. *Too many things happening?* "So you think—"

"Hold on, sweetie," Benjamin said as he snatched his ringing phone from his jacket pocket. "Benjamin Graham," he said, standing and taking a few steps from the table. "Yeah? So is this happening now? Damn! See, this has to stop—and I mean yesterday!" Benjamin paced the hallway. "Look, I'm on my way now. We're just going to have to figure this thing out. We can't just wait with our . . . holding our crotches. Tell everyone to be in my office in thirty minutes."

He walked back to Pam, pointing at his cell phone. "See what I mean? These guys can't pick their nose without asking me which finger to use. Your boy Alexander has it all figured out working for the Mazarredos. He got lucky being raised by that family, and they got lucky he's so involved."

Pamela suppressed a groan.

"When are you going to stop bouncing all over the world with this Formula One crap and come help me?" he continued. "Why would you want to work for someone else's business when you could be working for your own family's?"

Pam shook her head. "Let's not get into this right now, Dad."

"Pam, you've got to pull your head out and start taking life seriously! I thought you would've grown out of this by now. Hell, you think that job you got is secure? Wake up, Pam! It's not—trust me on that. You know whose job is safe at that company? The members of the family that runs it!"

Pam could see the veins popping in his forehead, and his face was now a deep burgundy. It happened every time the subject of her working at Graham Publishing came up.

"I said we're not getting into this right now, Dad."

"Oh yeah, well when will we? When the company's been run into the ground because you were too stubborn to take up the family business?"

Pamela was fuming, but she managed to keep her anger inside. She was relieved when his phone rang for the third time in ten minutes. *Saved by the bell.*

"What?" he snarled into the phone. "How many points? Are you sure? . . . Goddamn it. At this rate, the whole damn thing is gonna crash in a few weeks! I'm on the way in." He shoved the phone back into his jacket and turned his attention back to Pam. "Look, we'll talk about this later—I have to run." He shook his head. "Jesus Christ, the whole damn world is falling apart!"

Benjamin pulled a thick pen out of his pocket and took an envelope from the pile of mail on the table. "Listen, I want you to come to the Donald Wynn rally with me. There's a lot at stake in this country, and I think it's important that you be there. I'm giving you my assistant's number—Liz can make all of the arrangements to fly you out to wherever I am."

He slid the envelope with the scribbled number across the table and clicked the pen closed. Pam saw that the letter at the top of her mail pile had caught his eye—the one with the wax seal. He snatched it out of the pile, his eyes tightening as he examined the gold lettering.

"What in the hell is this?" he demanded.

Pam shrugged. "No idea. It just came in the mail the other day."

"You're saying you don't know anything about this?" Benjamin thrust the envelope toward her in accusation.

Pam crossed her arms. "No, I don't! Is that a problem?"

Benjamin crumpled the envelope and tossed it into the trash can. "No— and let's keep it that way!" He then marched down the hallway toward the door. "Don't forget to call Liz—and do it tomorrow, Pam!"

"But I have to pack for China, Dad!" she called after him.

Benjamin either hadn't heard her or pretended not to as he stormed out the front door. Rather than follow him and start a screaming match, she dropped into one of the dining room chairs and slapped her hand on the table. Across the room, she saw the envelope perched at the top of the trash can. *What was it about that letter that has gotten you so spooked?*

Pamela walked over to retrieve it but stopped when her BlackBerry began chirping a familiar melody. It was a selection from the Polovtsian Dances by Russian composer Aleksandr Borodin—a favorite of hers and Alex's. She'd designated it as his ringtone.

"Hey, Alex!" she answered. "My dad was over here a few minutes ago and we were just talking about—"

A voice, not that of Alex, interrupted her. "Ms. Pamela? This isn't Alex. It's his friend Li. I'm afraid Alex has had an accident."

CHAPTER 11

The black stretch limo made its way around the winding, picturesque path that led to the entrance of the Wynn National Golf Club. Various members of the press waited in a roped-off section set up just outside a colonial-style clubhouse. The limo circled the stone water fountain and pulled to a stop in front of the gathered reporters, camera crews, and guests.

The driver walked to the rear of the limo and opened the door. Wynn stepped out into a barrage of camera flashes in a dark-blue tailored suit, his signature pink tie traded for one in presidential blue. Wynn was looking more like the future leader of the free world every day.

He shook a few hands and posed for a few pictures before making his way to the podium set up on a makeshift platform on the green. The audience took their seats in the rows of folding chairs set up outside the clubhouse. This was intended to be the warm-up before the much larger production scheduled for a week later at the Walter T. Wallace Convention Center.

Wynn gave the audience a broad smile. "Thank you guys for coming out. First of all, is this a beautiful place or what? I'm not going to make this long, but wanted to share a few thoughts with you before tonight. As of right now, oil prices have doubled in one week, trillions of dollars are being moved in a sole effort to weaken the US dollar, and the market has dropped forty percent in less than eight days." Wynn paused to let the words sink in. "I have gotten reports that in some areas gas is selling as high as eight dollars a gallon. Curfews are being enforced to try to get a grip on the looting that has already started—you've all seen the reports. I mean, what am I saying? You guys are the ones reporting this stuff. I don't have to tell you!"

This drew light laughter from the crowd. Wynn paused as he caught the eye of *World News* reporter Grace Collins. A month earlier, she had been forced to take a leave of absence after taking a blow to the head. She'd been hospitalized after a flying glass bottle hit her during a live report on widespread looting in Detroit.

"Hello, Grace. Good to see you back," Wynn said. Grace smiled and nodded appreciatively.

"Listen, guys, we don't need to be going through this. Here are the hard facts; it's not going to get any better. The current administration is going to wait till gas prices hit ten dollars a gallon, the Dow hits two thousand, and the dollar is the equivalent of the peso before they try to do anything. And guess what? By then, it'll be too late!"

Wynn leaned over the podium and pointed at the live cameras. "I, like many of you, have worked too damn hard to allow this administration to run the country we love into the ground! They allowed China to treat us like fools . . . our gas prices to soar . . . the Dow to collapse . . . and I'll be damned if they're gonna get another four years to do it again!"

This drew a long a round of applause that drowned out the questions shouted by several reporters.

One of the guests stood among the reporters, watching Wynn's every move. Unlike most, she hadn't been invited. Once the assembly was over, she made her way to the parking lot, locked herself in her rented Ford Fusion, and made notes on a small pad. When she was finished, she had a brief summary of the number and descriptions of the bodyguards who flanked Wynn.

Zhao Xin had been trailing Wynn from the moment she arrived in the States. Because of her gender, security tended to be more lenient with her. Regardless, she was ready to do whatever was required to complete her mission. After getting a good assessment of the men around Wynn, there was little doubt that she could accomplish whatever President Bin needed.

A portly security guard who doubled as a parking-lot attendant tapped his flashlight against the fender of Zhao's rental and approached the driver's-side door. Zhao glared at the overzealous worker, holding back the temptation to swing the car door open and into his gut.

"Hey, Jackie Chan! We need to clear the parking lot. Can you get this rice burner moving?"

Zhao lowered her head and closed her eyes to do a short meditation. It was an exercise she'd been taught at an early age to control her temper. She opened her eyes and forced a smile.

Zhao put the car into reverse and backed out of the lot. As she passed the attendant, she looked at him one more time. He eyed her back, his hairy arms folded defiantly over his gut.

Last time she'd felt this insulted, two men died, one from a throat punch and the other from a sleeper hold that snapped his neck. She was almost aroused by the mere idea of getting out of the car and unleashing her fifteen years of training on this loser, but she held back. It was so tempting, but she was proud of her newfound control. Still she prayed that she would bump into the security guard again.

For now, she had a bigger target. With one call from her president, she could release some of the pent-up anger that never seemed to fully escape from within.

The anger, after all, did have its high points. She was angry on the very first day she met President Bin, the day he had attended the karate tournament finals in Beijing. Her skills were so advanced that they allowed her to compete against the men. The very same guy who was mocking her the day before ended up as her last opponent. The match ended in a record fifty-two seconds. She came out with her fifth karate tournament title, her opponent with a dislocated leg and a broken nose.

After the match, President Bin wanted to personally congratulate her. The next day he offered her a job as his bodyguard. After accepting the position, she moved from her one-room studio apartment to a room in the presidential palace.

CHAPTER 12

Pamela felt numb as she eased back into the dining room chair. *Alex in an accident? Is he okay? Has he died?*

Questions crisscrossed in her head, colliding together into a lump of total confusion. She couldn't find the words to ask what she knew she had to ask.

"Ms. Pam?" Li's voice said on the other end of the line. "Ms. Pam, you still there?"

"Yes, yes, I'm here. Is he okay?"

Li paused for far too long. "Yes and no."

"Come on, Li. Just blurt it out. What happened?"

Li told Pamela everything. He started from the beginning, with their plan to meet up in Pamplona and run with the bulls, and led up to the moment when things went wrong. He even confessed that they had disguised it as a business trip, knowing that their parents would never allow the excursion otherwise. Li's story was that he was meeting with investors in Madrid, while Alex didn't have to come up with much of a fib; Jorge was away on a three-week trip to Australia.

"He's going to be okay, Ms. Pam," Li finished. "But I feel responsible. I'm the one who pressed Alex to do this."

"Don't beat yourself up over it," Pam said before he could go on. "Alex is old enough to make his own decisions. I'm just glad you two are all right."

"Thanks. The doctor's here and wants to talk to you. I'll see you soon—and don't worry, I'll take care of Alex."

"Thanks, Li." She couldn't muster even a bit of anger, even though she couldn't imagine how crazy you'd have to be to try to outrun a stampede of raging bulls.

"*Hola, soy el doctor Herrera,*" said a throaty, amiable voice. *¿Eres le madre de Alexander?*"

"Yes. This—" Pamela paused. "*Sí, soy Pamela. ¿Esta bien Alex?*"

"English is fine," the doctor replied. "Don't worry, your son will be fine. I have been practicing here in Pamplona for over seven years and I have seen far worse than this. Looks like the bull speared him in the leg pretty good, but we were able to stitch that up. He also had a deep bruise on his thigh and another deep laceration on his arm. He lost some blood, but his friend here happened to be a match and donated some. He will be back to normal in a few days' time."

"Thank God," Pam said.

"From what he told me, I suspect that he also pulled a hamstring, which is why he fell in the first place. He got a little beat up, but this could have turned out a whole lot worse. Your son is very lucky."

Pam closed her eyes, unable to consider what could've happened. "Thank you so much, Doctor. Now that I know he's going to be okay, stand by—I'm about to come to Spain myself and kill him!"

Dr. Herrera laughed. "Don't be too hard on him. I did the same thing many years ago and almost got trampled. *Los chicos serán siempre chicos,* right?"

Pam smiled. "I suppose you're right, Doctor. Boys *will* be boys, but boys can also be boneheads. Can you put him on?"

"Sure. He will need to rest here for at least another day before he can go home, but if there is anything I can do, please let me know."

"Thank you again, Doctor!" said Pam, genuinely surprised by his thoughtfulness.

"My pleasure, Mrs. Pamela."

"Not that it matters, but it's Ms., not Mrs."

The doctor paused. "Is that right? I had a long conversation with your son when he came in. He was so worried about telling you, but he told me all about you. I apologize . . . I just assumed there was a Mr. Mazarredo, and—"

"Wait—hold on there, Doctor. I'm not a Mazarredo either, but that story is way too long to tell on an international call."

"Oh, you're in Texas, right?"

"You got it."

"Well, I do hope to meet you when you come to pick up your son, Ms. Pamela."

Is he flirting with me? Pam asked herself.

"You too, Doctor."

There was a pause, and then Alex was on the line. "Hey, Pam," he said sheepishly.

"Alex! Good lord! What in the world were you thinking? The running of the bulls? Really?" Pam stopped the lecture. "Alexander, I'm not trying to be the bad guy here, but you're smarter than that. Anything could have happened."

"Oh, you *are* upset, aren't you?"

"What do you mean?"

"Calling me Alexander? My entire name? It was sort of obvious."

Pamela laughed despite herself. "Oh, Alex, I guess you're right. I'm a little upset. Did you call Jorge yet?"

"No, not yet," said Alex, hesitating. "That's . . . that's why I had Li call you . . . You know, sorta hoping he didn't have to know."

"This isn't like the little mishaps you and Li got into in college. If Jorge found out that I kept something like this from him, he would kill me—and I could hardly blame him."

"No, really," Alex pleaded. "It'll be okay. Jorge's in Australia for the next three weeks. He'll teleconference into a few calls with me, but by the time he gets back I'll be totally healed. It would just worry him anyway."

Pam shook her head. "I can't believe you're talking me into this."

"Thanks!"

"Wait just a second, bull runner. I didn't say yes yet. I need to see how bad it is first, and—"

"It's not that bad at all," Alex blurted out. "The doctor said—"

"Alex, Alex, Alex—listen! I'm gonna have to see that handsome face of yours before I feel comfortable about this. I should be able to make it there by early morning at the latest. Got it?"

"Yep. And hey, how long are you going to be in town? Dad's letting me run an investors meeting for him in Madrid on Wednesday. You could come if you wanted."

"I'd love to."

"Perfect," he said. "I can't wait to see you. Oh, and I don't think I'm the only one."

"What does that mean?" asked Pam.

"Well, ever since I showed Dr. Herrera a picture of you, he won't shut up about wanting to meet you."

* * *

An hour after she hung up with Alex, Pam had made all the arrangements for her last-minute trip to Spain. In two hours, her plane would depart from Dallas. She reviewed her checklist, reciting each item aloud. *Left a message asking Roxy to keep an eye on my apartment. The cab to the airport on the way. Called the concierge to come up and help me with my bags. Got Formula One to change my itinerary. All packed for a week.*

She placed the last carry-on bag with the others by the door. As she thought about the contents of the three bags, she wondered if it was going to be enough. *Maybe I should have taken and extra pair of—*

Pamela jumped as the doorbell pealed through the apartment.

It's just the concierge, Pamela. You have to stop freaking out every time you have a visitor.

Pamela moved down the hall and lifted her eye to the peephole. There was the face of the concierge, fish-eyed by the glass. She unbolted the lock, turned the knob, and pulled. *I hope he brought the dolly.*

When the door opened, it was not the concierge who stood before her. Her words caught in her throat.

The man in her doorway stood well over six feet tall, left hand cuffed over right wrist in a stiff, official pose. His suit was dark and tailored, his stiff blond hair was parted neatly at the side, and his shoes looked far too expensive for any member of the concierge staff. His angular features betrayed no emotion. Something in Pamela's brain clicked. Three days before—the man outside the elevator. It was the same suit, the same build . . . the same man.

Pamela leaned to the side to see around his wide frame. Behind him stood another man in similar dress. With one hand, the other man gripped the upper arm of the horrified concierge, a frail man in his early thirties weighing no more than 155 pounds. Pam was sure he'd been at the Bonaventure for no more than three weeks.

Without a word, she turned her head back into the apartment, assessing her chances of getting to the silver vase. As if he could read her thoughts, the man at her door stepped across the threshold and gave her a knowing look: *Lady, don't even try it.*

CHAPTER 13

Beads of perspiration gathered on Pamela's forehead as she backed away from her massive visitor. Blocking the door with his body, the man slowly moved inside.

Her eyes shifted wildly for a way out. She tried to calm herself by turning her attention to his body language, searching for any sign of weakness that would allow her to bolt through the door. The stranger was not about to let that happen.

Once the blond man was inside, he turned back to his counterpart, who remained in the outside hallway, his hand locked on to the frail arm of the concierge. Pamela's intruder gave the other man a curt nod just before he closed and locked the front door. Pamela and the stranger were now alone.

"Let's move to another room," he said. "We need to talk to you briefly, Ms. Graham. It won't take long."

Pamela's mind raced with escape plans, but she followed his directions. There was no way she could overpower him, so obeying orders seemed like the smartest strategy for now. She led him down the hallway in measured steps as the man trailed close behind her. Halfway down the hall, she slowed her pace.

"Please move away from the vase, Ms. Graham. I don't want you getting any ideas."

Pam's shoulders slumped. *How could he possibly have known . . .*

They stopped in the dining room. The man walked over to the arched entry to the living area and gave the room a quick inspection. Seemingly satisfied, he turned his cold eyes back to Pam.

Pamela planted her feet in the carpet and crossed her arms, determined not to let fear get the best of her. *Okay, Pam, whatever is gonna happen is gonna happen.* For some reason, her intuition told her that she was safe. It was a tempting notion, even if her rational mind had a hard time grasping it.

"Listen," she said, "I don't know who the hell you think you are, but you'd better start talking right now."

As she spoke, she stared hard into the living room behind his shoulder. As expected, he couldn't help but look and see what was taking up so much of her attention. In the split second his head was turned, Pam quietly snatched the letter opener off the table and concealed it at her side.

The man locked his beady black eyes on Pam, seeming to analyze the scene in front of him rather than actually see it. He glanced at the table and then back at Pam.

"Where'd that letter opener go, Ms. Graham?" he said with a smirk. "I can guarantee you that an attack on me is ill advised. We are here on behalf of your government, not to harm you. A violent action on your part may sadly end any prior agreement I had for you to remain . . . unharmed."

Pam gripped the letter opener even tighter. "I'm supposed to trust that you won't harm me? If you actually know as much as you seem to, *agent,* you should also know that trusting the people you represent is *not* something I have any reason to do."

"Of course. We know all about your past differences with . . . certain organizations, Ms. Graham. But this is a different time, a different administration."

"Well, I'm seeing all the same callousness," Pam retorted. "You're invading my home, for God's sake."

He shot her a warning glare. "Ms. Graham, you're intelligent enough to know that we're not all cut from the same cloth." He finally unlocked his hand from around his wrist and showed her his palms in a less-than-convincing display of harmlessness. "Besides, I'm just the messenger."

His gesture caused his jacket to fall open slightly. Pam pointed to the left side of his chest. "A messenger who carries a gun?"

He looked down quickly. There was no gun showing, but now Pam knew without a doubt that he was carrying one. The second he realized he had been duped, the agent's attitude changed—and not for the better.

"You'll want to take all this very seriously, Ms. Graham," he said, buttoning his jacket. "I suggest you listen very closely to what I've been sent to tell you."

Her grip on the letter opener relaxed. She had taken her best shot at pissing him off, and he hadn't shot her. "Let's hear it," she said.

He jerked his sleeve up to check his watch. "We've already wasted a lot of time, so I'll make this quick. We know that you're on the way to Spain. I'm assuming that your Formula One assignment in China is still in place after that?"

"What business of yours is that?"

The agent held up his hand. "The questions I ask are not actually questions, Ms. Graham. Think of us as lawyers. We only ask questions we already know the answer to. First of all, we want you to be fully aware that you've been monitored for some time now and have been officially cleared of any involvement."

Pam frowned. "Involvement in what, exactly? Am I to assume, since you still haven't told me, that you're a representative of the CIA?"

"As to the second part of your question, in a word, yes. As to the clearing of your name—well, we decided we need your help. We've come across some information that certain parties in your small circle may be sharing secure information with non-ally countries."

Pam took a step closer to the agent. "This is a joke, right? Are you really trying to tell me that you think one of my friends is selling out my country?"

"We do not *think*, Ms. Graham."

Pam laughed lightly. "Oh, that's rich! I can truly say you guys are *way* off on this one."

"Are we? Be honest, Ms. Graham. Do you really know everything about the people in your life? That includes your semi-adopted son there in Spain, your friends in the US, the acquaintances you pick up on Formula One trips." He tilted his head to one side. "That reminds me: Did you ever tell him?"

Pam took a step back. "Tell who what?"

"You can drop the games with us, Ms. Graham." He stepped closer. "A little over a decade ago, something strained your relationship with your father. What was it exactly?"

This chilled Pam to her core. She remembered the agent's own words: *We only ask questions we already know the answer to.* She hadn't ever confronted her father about seeing him drive through the gates of the Bonham Grove conference all those years ago.

Her legs felt weak, and she leaned back against the table.

"What do you want from me?"

For the first time, a smile crept across the agent's face. "It's simple, Ms. Graham. We just want you to be observant for us. We will call you from time to time to question you about certain people. You will maintain your normal schedule. Nothing will change on your part. We just need you to keep your eyes and ears open."

Pam lowered her head in thought. "Who am I supposed to be watching?"

"I'm afraid I can't tell you at this point in time. Let's just say that the matter is serious, and may be closer to you than you think."

Pam heard the front door open. The agent turned and she followed him down the hall. The concierge stood in the entry with the second agent.

As they approached, the blond agent addressed the concierge—"Chris," read his name tag. "We're very sorry we had to involve you in this private matter. We'd really appreciate if you just pretended we were never here."

The second agent placed a heavy hand on the shoulder of the pallid concierge and spoke with a heavy Greek accent. "I think you know how to be discreet, don't you Chris?"

He nodded instantly, eyes fixed on the floor.

"Of course you do," the blond agent said with a humorless smile. "Now go ahead and get Ms. Graham's things down to her cab so she won't miss her flight." He passed Chris something that looked like a fifty-dollar bill, then watched him load the luggage to the cart and scurry to the elevator.

"All right, Ms. Graham," the agent said when the concierge was gone. "We'll be in touch." He stepped through the door with the Greek agent but turned and held it open for one final comment. "I think Alexander is doing better now—I wouldn't worry too much. Have a good flight, Ms. Graham."

When they were gone, Pam sat on the edge of her couch. Still in shock, she massaged her forehead with the tip of her fingers for a few minutes. When she'd regained a normal breathing rate, she stood, pushed the blond hair from her face, and made her way to the front door.

Five minutes later, she reentered the apartment. She rushed to the trash can, pulled out the wax-sealed envelope that had so upset her father, and placed it in her purse.

CHAPTER 14

The chauffeured Lincoln Town Car traveled south on Griffin Street, crossed over Elm, and turned right onto Main. The driver pulled to the curb in front of the Bank of America tower, the tallest building in downtown Dallas. The offices of Graham Publishing occupied the entire seventh floor of the skyscraper.

Benjamin Graham stepped out onto the sidewalk and walked inside with a brisk gait. As he exited the elevator onto the seventh floor, the chatter fell to a soft murmur. Employees shuffled papers and typed furiously as he whisked past them to the conference room.

The four heads of Graham Publishing sat at the glass-topped table, glancing nervously at one another.

"We all know what's happening here," Benjamin said, laying his briefcase on the floor and taking a seat in a swivel chair at the head of the table. "Now let me hear some theories on how the hell this happened." He took a big swig of his Voss water.

No one wanted to speak first. Benjamin closed his eyes tightly and pinched the bridge of his nose. A migraine—doubtlessly stress related—had been building in his head all morning.

He spoke with his eyes still shut. "Looks like I'm going to have to do the talking. We're going to have to start making some drastic steps to get this bleeding under control, guys. Nobody's buying papers, and our electronic offerings are hemorrhaging profits. We might be able to handle this if the economy weren't tanking, but I'll be damned if I'm going to ride all of my stock till it dwindles down to pennies."

Benjamin snatched a report on the table in front of him. It contained all the same numbers he'd heard on the phone call, but it was still difficult to accept. "Oil's up to damn near two hundred dollars a barrel in one week? Am I really reading this?"

The four executives swapped more helpless looks, rearranging their files as if some magical solution were hidden inside.

Benjamin turned his stare to his COO, David Jenkins. "David! Isn't it your job to keep an eye on the foreign markets? How in the hell was China able to practically disown the US dollar without me getting a heads-up from you?"

David slid a finger between his neck and collar and loosened his tie. He coughed lightly into his fist. "Ahem . . . sir, I . . . I'm just afraid that we didn't see it coming. I mean, no one saw it coming."

"Is that right? No one saw it coming? Then what in the hell has Wynn been ranting about for the past three years! Sure as hell looks like *he* saw it coming!" Benjamin rubbed his blocky chin in mock thought. "Oh, but maybe you're right. I was talking with my favorite waitress down at Murray's, and she never once mentioned that China going to trash the dollar and turn my stock into toilet paper!"

Benjamin stood, paced over to David's chair, and patted him on the shoulder. "If she didn't know, how could I expect you to?" He now clenched David's shoulder and shoved him backward with a grunt.

Benjamin stood over David like a bear ready to maul its prey and shoved a finger into David's face. "I guess the only difference is that I'm not paying a goddamn Murray's waitress six goddamn figures!"

"Mr. Graham?" said a female voice. Elizabeth, Benjamin's new personal assistant—his third in four months—stood at the door.

"What!" Benjamin said, not looking away from David.

Elizabeth hesitated before delivering the message. "Sir, I'm very sorry to bother you, but I have an urgent call on hold for you."

"Damn it, Liz! Take a message!"

"Sir, it's your daughter . . . and you told me to come get you—"

"I hope like hell that all of you bastards have your resumes updated," Benjamin said to the men, seething. "The second my daughter comes aboard, I'm gonna get rid of every single one of you!"

Benjamin flew to the door. David and the other men sat in their chairs like statues, stunned.

In his office, Benjamin slammed the door behind him and snatched up the phone. He jammed down the button next to the blinking red light. "Pamela?"

"Dad, it's me. I'm not going to be able to meet you tomorrow. I have to take a last-minute trip out of the country."

Benjamin gripped the phone. "That's bullshit, Pam, and you know it! I'll be in DC tomorrow, and you'd damn well better be there, too. This is not a good time to try and slip away from this, understand?"

"I understand, but—"

"There is no *but,* Pam! DC tomorrow. Period!"

Benjamin pressed a button and clicked over to his assistant's intercom. "Elizabeth! My daughter's on line four. Make the arrangements to get her to DC tomorrow."

He hung up without waiting for a response, but the phone bleated its ring as soon as he'd slammed it down on the base.

"Mr. Graham," said Elizabeth's voice, "before I set up your daughter's trip, you have a call on line three."

"Who is it?" he asked gruffly.

"She . . . she wouldn't say, sir. But she said it was vital that she speak with you."

Benjamin rolled his eyes. "All right, Liz. Put her through." There was a click. "Benjamin Graham speaking."

"Hello, Mr. Graham," said the voice of an elderly woman. "I'm going to keep this short, but I have information that's very important to get to you."

"Information? In reference to what?"

"Several things, actually. I recently saw you do an interview on CNN, and you had a lot to say about the economy, and your views on China were very insightful. Basically, I have a former colleague who I think is out to destroy you."

"What the hell are you talking about? Who is this?"

"I just need to meet with you, Mr. Graham." Something in her tone told him this woman wasn't messing around.

"When and where?"

"Are you going to be at the Wynn rally next week?"

"Yes."

"So will I. Let's meet in DC, then."

"I hope you realize that I'm a busy man. This won't go well if you're wasting my time. And I won't be giving you any money, whoever you are."

"There's no charge, Mr. Graham. This matter concerns your affiliation with a certain group. I need you to take information to someone—to warn them."

"Warn them, huh?"

"Yes," she said. "If you give me your cell phone number, I'll text you my name and contact information. Just call me when you get to DC. If we don't meet, something terrible could happen."

Benjamin spent nearly half of every day on the phone, and the tone of this woman's voice was unmistakable: She was scared to death.

"I'm transferring you back to my assistant," he said. "Just leave your information with her."

CHAPTER 15

Pam exited the rotating glass doors of her apartment building just as the badly shaken concierge loaded the last bag into the trunk of the cab. Chris refused to make eye contact with her as she walked toward the taxi and fell back into the backseat. He stood watching her from the safety of the lobby until the driver pulled into the street.

Pam's heart went out to the concierge; his frightened eyes reminded her of the way Alex had looked back at the orphanage in St. Petersburg. In fact, Chris probably looked a lot like she did during her terrified flight from Russia so long ago. Now he too had been jolted from a time of care-free innocence.

She asked the driver to turn on the radio as they pulled onto the Dallas North Tollway and headed south toward DFW International Airport. A report from NPR came through the speakers.

"In international news, new Chinese tax policies may drastically affect Europe's already struggling economy. The new agreement, drafted by the Chinese government, places a tax on the pipeline transport, likely restricting the flow of gas into Russia. Analysts say that this move will cause a major energy and heating crisis in Western Europe in the upcoming winter months.

"In other news, China, the number-two economic power in the world, is now said to be in talks with Venezuela to take over the control of that country's vast oil shipments to the United States. What does this mean for the US? It means a lot. Should China reroute these shipments, the move could essentially prevent approximately one and a half million barrels a day from coming into the US and put a severe strain on its oil supply.

"And presidential candidate Donald Wynn will be in Iowa today, hoping to—"

The driver lowered the volume. "Crazy, huh?"

Pam looked up to see him staring at her through the rearview mirror. All she could see were his dark, bushy eyebrows and twinkling brown eyes. His dark Middle Eastern features were weather beaten, but he looked friendly. He gave her a conspiratorial smile.

Like most taxi drivers, Pam guessed that the smile and small talk were part of the cabbie's strategy for pushing the gratuity up as far as possible.

"I'm sorry, what was that?" Pam asked.

"I say, 'Crazy, right?' You know, time we are in, money problems, oil . . . all crazy. I make fifteen dollars all day yesterday, and you ask me why?"

No, I actually didn't, Pam thought.

"I tell you! Gas prices! No joke, you believe it? 'S killing me. Market down, business down . . . nobody needs taxi. My brother drives cab in Virginia—same thing. No good."

Pam smiled and nodded but turned her attention to her phone. She could feel him eyeing her in the mirror as she pretended to type a message.

"You hear about credit drop, right?"

Pamela brought the phone close to her face in an exaggerated performance of sending a text message.

"The Dow drops for the tenth day in a row," said the barely audible voice on the radio.

"Hello?" he said, switching the newscast off entirely. "You hear about how they drop our credit rating? You think will take America to a, um . . . depression?"

Pam sighed loudly and ended her make-believe text. "Looks like you want to talk politics, huh, Mr. Driver?"

She couldn't see his mouth in the mirror, but could see the smile in his eyes. *Ease up, Pam. Engaging this guy in a short conversation isn't gonna kill ya. So far he's far more knowledgeable than Roxy.*

"You want my opinion?" she said.

He nodded enthusiastically. "Yes, please."

"A depression isn't likely since we're going into an election year. But it *is* looking pretty grim about now. It feels like everything is going against us at the same time. But we'll have to wait and see what happens."

He nodded. "This is true."

"But honestly, I'm not too worried," Pam added. "We sort of have a leg up, since the dollar is the world's currency."

The conversation wound down from there. The driver concentrated on the road, seemingly lost in his own thoughts. Pamela quickly tossed the political thoughts aside and was soon back to mentally replaying her conversation with the CIA agent. She'd always regarded government agents as goons, pawns in the diabolical schemes the country's leaders yearned to perpetrate against the citizens. But what if they were telling the truth this time? Was someone around her involved in something sinister? What kind of information did any of her friends have that would put national security at risk?

The cab passed through the last airport tollbooth, then curved around to terminal C. At the curb, the skycap approached the car as the driver unloaded the trunk. Pam stepped out, tipping the skycap and the driver.

"Thank you, Ms. Graham," said the cabbie.

Pam smiled back. "You're welcome. It was nice chatting with you."

He paused before pulling the handle on the driver's-side door. "Oh, and about the dollar, I think I would have to say . . . for now."

Pamela cocked her head to the side. "I'm sorry. For now?"

"Yes. You know, the talk in the car about the dollar," he said.

Pam wasn't following. She had too much on her mind already.

He smiled and explained. "You said that the dollar is the world's currency. So I just say, for now." He lowered his head, opened the door, and folded himself into the driver's seat.

Pam stood at the curb as the cab sped away, pondering the driver's parting words. Perhaps he was right, though the prospect filled Pam with dread.

Inside the spacious, light-filled airport, her eyes were drawn to a man sitting just outside the coffee shop, facing the main entrance. Realizing he'd been spotted, the man lifted his *USA Today* to cover his face. The polo shirt, the khakis, the penny loafers—it was such a blatant effort to blend in that he ended up standing out more than he would've in his dark suit.

Something came over Pamela, perhaps the pressure from a decade of unvented anger. Before she knew it, she was walking directly toward him.

CHAPTER 16

"Anything interesting in the news today?"

The man lowered the newspaper and looked up at Pam, perplexed. He opened his mouth but failed to find the right words.

Pam leaned over the top of the paper to see what he was reading.

"The entertainment section, huh? How *is* the new Justin Bieber album?"

Blood rushed to the man's cheeks. He stared into the crowd. It wasn't either of the men who'd been at her place, but she had a hunch, and his reaction was proving her right.

"Expecting someone?" she asked. "Wait . . . Hold on a second—you were waiting for me, weren't you? Well, tell your guys I'm sick to death of this. If I see one more of you thugs staring at me, things will get ugly. And you'd sure as hell better not be getting on flight 1356 with me."

She stomped off to the ticket counter, astonished at her performance. When she turned around less than a minute later, the agent was gone.

* * *

"Don't get yourself worked up, Liz," Pam said once she'd taken a window seat on the plane. "Trust me, I know more than anyone that my dad doesn't take no for an answer, but I'll take all the blame for this one."

Pam heard the sigh of relief from Benjamin's assistant over the hum of the airplane passengers around her. Now that she was on her flight to Spain, meeting her dad in DC was now an impossibility.

"What should I tell him, though?" Elizabeth asked. Her voiced cracked as if she were on the verge of tears.

"Take my advice and don't let my dad get to you, okay? I'm sure you already know about how he goes through assistants like toilet paper. The reason they don't last isn't because of them; it's because they stick out like sore thumbs. They try to do too much, and that annoys Dad. Just do whatever he asks and stay invisible, know what I mean?"

"Yeah, I think so."

"Think of it this way," Pam continued. A gaudily made-up woman took the seat next to her, filling the area with the scent of cheap perfume. "Working for my dad is like lighting the fuse on a stick of dynamite. You do your job and light the damn thing, and then get the hell out of the way."

Elizabeth giggled. "That's a good way to put it."

"There you go! That's all you need to know. I'm on my way to Spain, so there's no way I'll make it to DC. Just go ahead and book my flight anyway, but make sure you pay extra for the cancellation option. After he finally accepts that I'm not going to show up, you can cancel it and get the money back. He'll blow his top, but not at you."

"Thank you so much, Pamela," Elizabeth said.

"Not a problem, Liz. Just keep lighting those fuses and getting out of the way. You'll be all right."

Pamela switched off her phone and leaned back against the headrest. She thought about her father's out-of-control temper, and about poor Alex, attacked by a savage bull. She rooted around in her cluttered purse, fishing until she found the scrap of paper with the hospital's address. There, among the lipstick tubes and packages of tissue, was the wax-sealed envelope, creased and wrinkled from her father's fist.

She pulled it out, devoting her full attention to it for the first time. The front displayed a New York PO box, and on the back was the wax seal, stamped with a logo: the letters *BG* in bold script, crisscrossed by palm trees.

What was it about this envelope that got you so spooked, Dad?

She broke the wax seal with a plastic pen from her purse and removed the card inside. The top corner of the invitation displayed a full-color version of the logo above the words "BRAZILIAN GROVE."

Angling the card away from her seatmate, who was now distractedly flipping through the pages of a dog-eared *Us Weekly*, Pamela read the elegant lettering.

> *Dear Pamela,*
>
> *We are pleased to inform you that you have been personally selected to receive this rare invitation to become a part of an exciting and elite group of women. The Brazilian Grove is an invitation-only women's social club. Founded in 1999 by Catherine Caddaric, a former executive of one of the biggest broadcasting networks in the world, we are located in the heart of New York City. We currently have 125 influential members from the military, financial, and diplomatic sectors.*
>
> *These invitations are sent to only a select number of women. We believe that you will not only benefit from becoming a member but will also become an asset to our club. If you choose to accept this invitation, we will be meeting in the nation's capital this year and will make all of the necessary arrangements for you.*
>
> *One of our members will be contacting you within the next week. Congratulations, and we are looking forward to meeting with you very soon.*
>
> *Sincerely,*
> *The Brazilian Grove*

Pam wrinkled her nose. She'd bypassed Girl Scout troops, high school cliques, and sororities, and she certainly had no interest in being any part of this Brazilian Grove, whatever it was.

She was about to recrumple the invitation when she had a thought. *Could this be related to the Bonham Grove?*

That was the only explanation for her father's anger. He'd recognized the seal and couldn't bear the thought of his baby girl joining such an organization. Was it because the Brazilian Grove was opposed to the Bonham Grove? Or were they related? Perhaps he feared she'd learn too much about his own involvement.

She placed the invitation back in her purse as the plane taxied toward the runway. She'd deal with it later.

CHAPTER 17

"Okay, here we are, sir. Ninth Street!" The cab driver got out amid a flurry of honking horns and rushed to the rear door. Benjamin Graham stepped out and twisted to one side. He'd been stiff as a board since he boarded the plane in Dallas.

He heaved one bag across his shoulder and pulled the other behind him on rollers. As he stepped up onto the sidewalk, he stubbed his toe against a partially raised manhole cover.

"Damn it!"

He stepped to the side of the thick iron circle and noticed a group of construction workers down the sidewalk who'd noticed his mishap. He shot them the finger, and they burst out in raucous laughter. Deciding to let it go, Benjamin continued on toward the Renaissance Washington Hotel with a slight limp.

Inside, Benjamin made his way straight to the front desk. "Any messages for Benjamin Graham?"

The concierge tapped a few keys and studied his screen. "No sir, I'm afraid not," he said in a crisp British accent. "But if any come in I will be sure to phone you straight away."

Once he was checked in and settled into his room, he poured himself a stiff scotch and dialed the number for his assistant.

"Where the hell is Pam?" he shouted as soon as she picked up. "I checked into my room an hour ago!" he lied. "According to the itinerary you forwarded me, Pam should've already been here."

"One second, sir," Elizabeth said. "Let me check."

He cradled the cell phone between cheek and shoulder as he twirled the scotch with a finger. While he listened to his assistant type on the other end of the line, Benjamin studied himself in the full-length mirror on the closet door. *My God, I'm aging.* Bluish veins protruded from his forehead, and his skin glowed crimson red. His hairline appeared to have receded half an inch overnight. His belt dug into the growing layer of fat around his waist.

"I can't find anything, sir. I have no idea why your daughter isn't there. I was certain she would be."

"You don't have any idea?" he spat. "Who the hell set up her travel plans?"

Elizabeth paused. "I did, sir."

"*Now* we're getting somewhere. Did you give her the correct information? Did you check to see if her flight left on time?"

"I gave her all the information. I told her over the phone, left her a message, e-mailed her the itinerary, and texted her. I just checked, and her flight left right on schedule."

"So what happened to her?"

Elizabeth remained quiet.

"*Hello?*"

"Well, my guess is . . . that she didn't get on the plane, sir."

Benjamin moved away from the mirror and flopped into a wide pearl-white chair. There was silence on the other end of the phone. He took several deep breaths. When he spoke again, he had regained control.

"Okay, Liz. I'll be here for at least a couple of weeks, so just try and keep the office together. I'll send for you if I need you here in DC." He was about to hang up when he remembered something. "Hey, do you have the name and number of the lady I transferred to you the other day?"

"Yes sir," Elizabeth said. "I saved them in your phone. I also wrote them down on a business card and put it in your wallet."

Benjamin pulled out his wallet. In the first credit card slot was a card with two letters and a number written across it. "So she didn't leave her full name?"

"No sir, just her initials."

"Good enough. I'll call you if I need anything."

"Yes sir."

"And Liz?"

"Sir?"

"Good job," he said in a low voice.

"No need to thank me, sir. It's my job." There was a click and she was gone.

Though the bar downstairs called to him, Benjamin willed himself to get some work done. He powered up his laptop to check the market, replied to several e-mails, and then typed a to-do list for his COO. He also checked Graham Publishing's stock; it was even worse than he anticipated. After staring at the numbers in disbelief, he slammed the laptop closed, overcome by fatigue.

He leaned back in the chair and closed his eyes, conjuring up happier, less stressful times. A memory from Pam's childhood resurfaced; they were together at a cart race, Pam not more than nine. It had been a mild day filled with laughter, even though Pam had been upset at taking second place to a teenage boy.

He still hoped she would turn up in DC, but he knew that was unlikely. Pam was the only one who knew how to calm him down. Just like her mother had before she passed away, Pam would scrunch up her nose when he said something she didn't like. That face alone was enough to lower his blood pressure several points. *Hell, Pam, where on earth are you?*

In his heart, he knew that Pam might never step into leadership at Graham Publishing. She was—according to her own reports, anyway—happy working at Formula One and had no intentions of leaving.

Benjamin came to an upsetting truth: *Looks like you need her more than she needs you, old man.*

* * *

Benjamin, stationed at the far end of the hotel bar, lifted his finger for another round. What was that—his fifth? Sixth? He'd lost track. Either way, the much-needed buzz proved elusive this evening.

He scowled at his persistent sobriety after each scotch. It was one of those days. There was too much on his mind, too much at stake, for the liquor to take effect.

When Benjamin sloshed down the last of the fifth or sixth drink, the bartender lifted his head and looked at Benjamin from across the room. Benjamin shook his head this time. The bartender made his way over.

"Ready to close out your tab, Mr. Graham?"

"Yeah, go ahead and close me out, kid." He stood and tossed a twenty on the bar. "This is for you. Charge the drinks to my room."

"Sure thing, Mr. Graham. You have a nice evening."

Benjamin buttoned his sport coat as he walked out, feeling in the pockets for his room key. He stopped when he saw a familiar head of cropped silver hair among a group of people at the end of the bar. *Well, I'll be damned. Look who's come out of her lair.*

Benjamin could feel his temperature rise as he made a beeline for her. This was just the outlet he needed for all his frustration.

Soon all eyes in the group of about ten people were focused on the flushed man striding angrily toward them. Looks of recognition came across several of the people, and the silver-haired woman who was his target looked to her left and right.

"That's right, Catherine!" Benjamin shouted. "You bet your wrinkled ass I'm here to talk to you!"

CHAPTER 18

B enjamin's loud declaration caught the ear of two members of hotel security. They rushed up and formed a wall between Benjamin and the silver-haired woman moments before he reached her.

"Mr. Graham, we need you to hold on right there for a minute," one of the men said.

The other one spoke into his two-way radio. "Available security staff, please report to the bar ASAP."

Benjamin looked at the guards and crossed his stout arms over his chest. At six foot three, he towered over the medium-build security guards. "You boys are kidding me, right? I tell you what, you got two seconds to get the hell out of my way, or I'm gonna slam you little punks into that table. You really think minimum wage is worth getting your asses kicked?"

The two men took a step back in unison as the woman behind them spoke. "That's okay, boys. This is an old friend of mine. He's just playing around."

The two men stared at her for a moment before stalking off together, embarrassed.

Benjamin's target stepped from the group, a glass of wine clutched in a vein-covered hand. She waved at her friends, signaling that there was nothing more to see. Still, several members of the group cast suspicious looks at Benjamin.

"Benjamin, my dear, we don't need to make a scene, now do we? What exactly is this all about?" Her tone was condescending and motherly, and it only stoked his already red-hot temper. He knew it was all an act. Behind closed doors, this woman was ruthless.

"Get off it, Catherine! You know goddamn well what I need to talk to you about!"

"Do I?"

Benjamin untwined his large arms and slammed a fist into the palm of his other hand. "You're so damn lucky you're a *woman*, Catherine. What in the hell are you doing sending my daughter an invitation to your witch club?"

Catherine lifted her eyes in mock surprise and placed her wine glass on a nearby table. When she spoke, her voice was like ice, all traces of the motherly tone gone. "Let's take this conversation to my suite, Mr. Graham."

* * *

Catherine Caddaric's presidential suite had an unobstructed view of the Wallace Convention Center. Standing before the wide window, she poured herself a glass of cabernet and held the bottle toward Benjamin. "Want some?"

"No."

Catharine arched an eyebrow. "You on the wagon now, Ben Graham?"

Benjamin shook his head. "Not here to chitchat, Cathy." He shoved his finger at her. "You crossed the line."

Catherine frowned. "What line, Ben? Pamela is a grown woman. She can make her own calls now, don't you think?"

"That's where you're wrong—dead wrong—and I'll be damned if I ever let her join that group of psychotic bitches you rule over!"

"Oh, come on now, Ben. We're above insults now, aren't we?"

"Look!" Benjamin yelled. "I don't want you ever contacting Pam again, understand? If you want to play show-and-tell, I have no problem exposing what you really are, Cathy. And believe me, when it comes to my daughter, I'm more than happy to play dirty. I've done plenty of digging on you and your girls, and I know what you're up to."

Catherine stepped closer to Benjamin like a cat taunting an enraged pit bull. "I'd stop right there, Benjamin. If I were you, I wouldn't say anything you'll regret later."

Benjamin squinted, trying to get a read on her. Her thin face was stern, her jaw clenched tight. If there was one thing everyone knew about Catherine, it's that she wasn't one to bluff. Failing to heed her warnings was a grave error, and many had learned the hard way.

"Let me tell you something, Cathy. I don't give a rat's ass what you do to me. You can take whatever you think you have on me and shove it right up your pasty, scheming ass!"

Catherine grinned, but her eyes remained deadly serious. She walked over to the window and looked down on the street below in silence, taking a sip of wine before she spoke.

"You're telling me you're willing to lose it all for your daughter not to join my organization? That's an easy thing to do when you don't know what's truly at stake, Ben. Sure, your mouth is saying that you're willing to pay any price, but I know better. I knew you when you were just an errand boy at your dad's little company. I watched you grow up there. I watched you take up the flag. You don't own Graham Publishing; you *are* Graham Publishing. Without it, you cease to exist. You'll do anything to keep it." Catherine twisted her head, feigning curiosity. "Am I wrong, Ben?"

Benjamin let his rage override the pit of fear in his stomach. "You're pressing the wrong buttons, Cathy. I'm getting the hell out of here, and trust me—it is for your sake, not mine. If I find out you've so much as looked at my daughter ever again, there will be hell to pay."

As he stormed to the door of her suite, Catherine delivered her final blow.

"Oh, and Ben—next time you see A. J., say hello for me, will you?"

Benjamin stopped, his hand wrapped around the doorknob. He was unable to hide his shock. Dizziness began to overtake him. His chest heaved in short, labored breaths. Until that very second, he'd been sure he would take that secret to the grave. Now the game had changed drastically.

Did she really just say A. J.? The name was like a gun aimed directly at his head.

Suddenly the reality of the situation appeared in his mind like a vision. In normal circumstances, Catherine would never have invited the granddaughter of Benjamin Graham Sr. to join her organization; he was positive of that. She felt bold enough to approach Pam because she had an ace up her sleeve.

Her words pounded in his head. *"Next time you see A. J., say hello for me."*

Oh my God in heaven, of all the people in the world, she *knows.*

CHAPTER 19

The rickety cab wound around Pamplona for a seemingly endless thirty minutes before Pamela spotted the hospital. The words "Hospital San Miguel" stood tall in brilliant blue letters atop the building. Gorgeous green glass covered most of the building's façade. She quickly shoved a handful of bills into the driver's hand and leapt out the car.

Inside, a large waiting area was filled with people. Pam spotted a woman in light blue scrubs standing behind the small semicircle of what she assumed was the information desk, and she started in her direction. Before she got there, she heard a man's voice call her name. She spun around to find a man wearing a doctor's lab coat and a warm smile.

"Hello, Ms. Pamela. You are here for Alexander, correct?"

Pamela nodded cautiously. "Uh, yes . . . How—"

"I have been taking care of your son."

The man extended his hand, and she clasped it in her own. Of course—his was the voice on the phone. Alex had shown him the photograph of her.

He continued shaking her hand and brought his other to rest on top of it. "Pardon me, I should have introduced myself. I am Dr. Herrera. We spoke on the phone."

"I thought that was you! It's a pleasure to meet you, Doctor. How's my kiddo doing?"

"Just a little sore. But he is young. He will be fine. And he is all ready to go home."

Pamela found herself drawn to the doctor's cordial manner, though she could feel his eyes look her body up and down.

"Doctor?" Pam said.

"Yes?"

Pamela gestured at her hand, which he still held with both of his.

A red glow surfaced on his cheeks as he released it and dropped his arms to his sides. "I am so sorry. Please let me take you to your son's room. He will be so happy to see you."

When Pam walked into the sparse but clean hospital room, Alex's eyes lit with excitement. Although he was much older now, he had the same adolescent face she'd fallen in love with years ago in Russia. He stood slowly from the cramped twin bed and hugged her tightly.

"Pam! You finally got here!"

"Hey, Alex!" Pam said, holding him at arm's length and looking him over. "You don't look bad at all! Are you feeling okay?"

"Honestly?"

Pam folded her arms. "Yes, honestly, and write this down—it's always honestly. Next time I want a dishonest answer I'll let you know."

Alex lifted his hands in surrender. "All right, all right. I get it. I'm okay I guess. My legs still feel a little tight, but the doctor said it'll go away soon."

"Good. No pain anywhere else?"

"No. Just feeling pretty . . . tired."

"I'm so glad you're okay, Alex. You scared me half to death."

Alex beamed back at her. "Yeah, well, I was pretty scared too when I saw that animal coming down on top of me."

"If your father had any idea—"

"Pam, you can't tell him." Pam gave him a stern look, but he continued before she could voice her doubts. "Let's just get out of here. Everyone's been great, but I'm more than ready to leave."

Pam helped pack Alex's few belongings into the bag Li had brought to him. As they were finishing up, Dr. Herrera came back in and stood before Pam, hands clasped eagerly in front of him.

"I would love to take you to dinner tonight, Ms. Pamela." He extended a business card with two fingers.

Pam took the card and smiled. "I'd love to take you up on that, but we're headed to Madrid tonight. It seems that my little adventurer here has a big meeting tomorrow." Pamela squinted at Alex in mock anger; he grinned and hunched his shoulders in return.

"Perhaps another time?" the doctor said.

"Sure, Doctor."

"Antonio. Please, call me Antonio," he insisted.

"You got it. And next time you're in Texas, lunch is on me."

"What, no dinner?"

Pam laughed. "Well, I'll be damned. I offer you lunch and you shoot for dinner!"

"Hey, why not?" he said.

"I guess it's true what they say—you never know until you ask."

"This is true. Which brings me to my next request. Think you can spring for my ticket to Texas?" He winked.

"You're on a roll today, Antonio! I'm gonna have to think about that one. Next time y'all get snow in the summer, I'll be sure to send for ya. Deal?"

"Ouch!" he exclaimed. "In all honesty, I may be in the States next week, but not Texas. There is a medical conference in Washington I paid to attend, but I'm still debating." He scratched the side of his face and raised an eyebrow at Pamela. "Now, if I could get a certain slim blonde to meet me for dinner while I was in town . . . well, that may convince me . . ."

Pam shook her head before he could finish. "You're swinging the hell out of that bat there, Antonio, but I'm afraid you've struck out again. I'll be in China next week."

Antonio shrugged and smiled. "Looks like bad timing. Story of my life."

CHAPTER 20

A lex's big meeting was to take place at the Eurostars Madrid Tower, and he'd invited Pam to accompany him. She had only a vague notion of Alex's new role in the company, and he was eager for her to see the respect he'd already garnered fresh out of Brown. He had urged her to come, saying it would be a small group and that no one would mind a visitor.

As the chauffeured limo, courtesy of Mazarredo Inc., pulled up to the hotel, Pam felt like she could run a mile. They'd taken a direct flight from Pamplona to Madrid the night before and had risen early to make the 9:00 a.m. meeting. Though they'd gone to bed late, she'd slept like she hadn't in months. The few hours of deep REM sleep felt like a short visit to heaven. Now that she was out of Dallas, she felt an inexplicable calmness.

Wearing a sharp skirt and jacket she'd deemed perfect for the meeting, she followed Alex into the towering cylinder of the hotel. Giant gold letters bearing its name curved across the front of the building, contrasting elegantly with the dark glass.

When they got to the hotel's lavish meeting room, a handful of men stood in clusters, chatting. The attendees seemed to be of almost every nationality Pam could think of. In front of two rows of chairs stood an elegant black podium, and behind it a screen displayed a projection of the Mazarredo logo and the word "WELCOME!"

Pam gestured for Alex to go on without her and hung back in the rear of the room close to two tables laden with hors d'oeuvres. On each table were silver platters filled with fresh fruit, small decorative cakes, and caviar with crackers. Despite the rumbling of her stomach, she resisted the temptation to grab a plate.

Watching the former Russian orphan mingle with businessmen twice his age, Pamela felt a twinge of pride. She was finally getting a chance to see Alex in action, making strides toward becoming the leader of his family's company. And he wouldn't even be twenty-one for a few more days—or at least something close to that. His birth certificate had never turned up.

You've come a long way, kiddo, she thought.

According to Alex, the thirteen guests consisted of the seven members of the Mazarredo board, a Russian investor, two investors from China, a diplomat from Venezuela, a representative from Kazakhstan's national oil company, and a hired speaker. Pamela took a seat on a bench and observed the small group, paying particular attention to the Chinese investors. She hoped to make a connection with them before heading to Beijing.

After a few minutes, a slender American dressed in a loose, cheap-looking suit began ushering the men into their seats. Pamela pegged him as just under fifty years old. As conversation died down, the man walked to the podium and rubbed his hands together. Not a single person had seemed to notice her sitting on the bench in the back of the room. For now, that was the way she wanted it. She was perfectly content to be a fly on the wall.

"Welcome," said the man, looking out at the men before him. "As you all know, my name is Steven Baxter, and I've been organizing these types of gatherings with Mazarredo for over sixteen years now. I'd like to take the opportunity to welcome each and every one of you—we're glad you all could make it." He seemed nervous and shifty. As he prattled on about the meeting, the hotel, current events, and a hodgepodge of other topics, he fidgeted with the papers before him and frequently glanced back toward the door. It was something more than speaker's nerves. His eyes had a far-away look, as if the tired observations and flat one-liners he was delivering were the last thing on his mind. *What's up with this guy?* thought Pam.

"Well, you guys aren't here to hear me ramble on," he said at last. No one at the table laughed. "How about we bring up the man who put this all together? I would like to introduce to you Alexander Dezcallar de Mazar-redo—or as we call him at the company, Jorgecito!"

The men applauded heartily as Alex stood and made his way to the front of the small crowd. His limp was there, but Pam was sure she only noticed because she was looking for it.

"I'm so happy that everyone made it here today," Alex said. Pam couldn't help notice how handsome he'd become, how dapper he looked in his dark-blue suit. "As you all know, my father is out of the country. In fact, he wanted me to tell everyone that if I screw up this meeting, he's going to reschedule it and buy everyone a drink at the bar." A burst of laughter came from the group. "And that's why I had the hotel staff leave a bottle of fine whiskey in each of your rooms. I figured that way, not only would I outdo his one drink, but even if I do screw this up, none of you will remember."

The men ate it up, laughing and cheering.

"On a more serious note, I do hope you enjoy your stay here. This hotel has always been a favorite of mine and my father's. And we are excited that we have a couple of investors from the People's Republic of China with us today." Alex pointed to them as they stood and bowed to polite applause.

Pam wondered what the other men in the room were thinking, given that China was the hot topic of the moment. Even Alex had expressed some concerns about the country's growing power and how they intended to use it. The night before, he'd told her that Li skipped out of Pamplona early following a heated discussion about his father's policies.

Alex continued to introduce the other guests, before launching into an overview of the company's recent activities and investments. Pamela marveled at how the shy, scrawny little boy she met over a decade ago had grown into such a well-spoken, intelligent young man. If she had any regrets about taking him out of Russia, they were gone in that moment. Being raised by her friends the Mazarredos couldn't have turned out better for him.

As she looked on from her seat next to the food tables, she noticed that Steven, the nerve-wracked speaker, cast occasional glances back in her direction. He seemed to be the only one who acknowledged her existence. *Not in this or even the next lifetime,* Pam thought after he turned to stare for a fourth time.

When Alex had finished up his state-of-the-company address, Pam slid out of the room as the group clapped. She'd listened to Alex with rapt attention, but she couldn't take another speech from a Steven Baxter type. For the next hour, she wandered the lobby, checking her mail on her phone and catching up on the news.

Pam reentered the meeting room when she heard a round of applause, correctly guessing that the meeting was breaking up. The men milled around, with the largest group gathered around Alex. Pam reclaimed her bench seat and watched the scene.

She averted her eyes as the obese Russian businessman waddled back to the food table, preferring to avoid a conversation with a stranger. The two Asian investors, one standing nearly a foot taller than the other, joined him after a few moments. Once the three of them had filled their tiny paper plates with food, they formed a tight circle a few feet from her. She pulled out her phone and scrolled through recent headlines, ears open.

The stubby Asian looked around before speaking. He spotted Pam and jerked his head in her direction. The Russian turned his obese body all the way around to take a look.

"Spanish hooker," he scoffed. "Don't mind her. She cannot understand English."

He turned his back to Pam and the men continued to talk as if she weren't even there. Pamela eyes bored into the back of the Russian's meaty head. The taller Asian glanced at her again, but Pam broke eye contact and went back to her phone.

"We will continue with deal we spoke of before meeting, yes?" the Russian was saying.

The Asian investors nodded their heads.

The Russian looked around periodically, speaking in guarded tones, but Pamela took in every single word. "I own investment business in Russia," he rasped. "I have heard your country make a tremendous amount of money off the Americans, yes?"

The Asian man nodded. "We make more than you can imagine," said one.

"They borrow much from you?" The Russian shoved two crackers into his mouth.

"Yes, they borrow more than any country, and will pay whatever interest we charge them." The shorter Asian man smiled and shook his head. "The Americans are not so smart."

"Yes, they are not wise," the Russian replied with a knowing smile.

The tall Asian investor continued. "We charge them very high rates, then make even more from what we export to them."

"So, you loan them same money you make from them?" The Russian shook his head in disbelief. "Unbelievable. Maybe we work together on this. Perhaps take to next level, something that make our ruble stronger."

The Asian investors shared a smile. "We just may be able to work as one on that," said the shorter one. "President Bin and I discussed this very matter just the other day."

The Russian businessman nodded eagerly. "Anything our countries do together is good, I think."

The three men touched glasses in a toast. "To new comrades," said the Russian.

The short Asian man looked over his shoulder before speaking. "Yes, but we do have one small concern."

"Yes?" the Russian asked. "What?"

"We are concerned that if a certain man comes into power in America, he may change the rules and make it difficult to proceed with our current arrangements."

The Russian placed his glass on the table. "So we wait. We see who is president before we move."

"It is only a small issue, anyway," said the tall Asian. "President Bin will never allow it to happen. We are all watching this man closely. If he wins"— the man placed his index finger to his temple, lowered his thick thumb, and expelled air to make the sound of a tiny explosion—"he loses."

The Russian grunted in laughter, but the three men suddenly seemed solemn. They traded meaningful looks, clinked their glasses together once more, and moved back to the group of other men without another word.

Pamela remained on the bench, wondering if she could've possibly heard what she thought she did. A numb sensation crept through her as she continued to stare at her BlackBerry.

When she looked back up, the three men had spread apart and were mingling with the group. The shorter Asian investor was chatting it up with

Steven, the first speaker, while his companion made his way to Alex. After they exchanged a few words, she saw Alex point her way. They began walking toward her.

"I'd like you to meet Pamela," Alex said as they approached.

Pamela stood.

"Who . . . who is this?" the man stuttered.

"This is my mother. I can't believe I've been so rude as to leave her sitting back here all alone."

The Asian locked eyes with her in a stare that bordered on menacing. "You . . . speak English?"

A grin spread across Alex's face. "Better than anyone here! She's a native Texan."

The Asian man's nostrils flared. He knew she'd heard every word.

CHAPTER 21

When Benjamin Graham woke up the next morning, his head felt like it was filled with cement. The empty bottle of Courvoisier stood next to a glass that was still half full of the dark, potent liquid. He grabbed his head with both hands and stared at the ceiling in a daze.

After a couple of failed attempts at standing, he managed to get on his feet. The room swam before his eyes. Incoherent thoughts ran through his head as he stumbled to the bathroom.

With a twist of the ivory lever, frigid water sprayed from the gold faucet, and he splashed his face a couple of times. As he washed, the monogrammed robe he didn't even remember putting on hung open, exposing his forty-eight-inch waist. Peering back at him in the mirror was an aged version of his former self. He pushed against the thick, leathery skin of his cheeks and then pulled back the skin at his temples to give himself a momentary facelift. The wrinkles and pouches reappeared as he released his face. "Hell, I look even more ancient than I did yesterday," he said aloud.

As he shuffled out of the bathroom, hazy memories of the evening before flooded back. He began pacing the length of the hotel suite, hands shoved deep in the pockets of the plush robe. He stopped to kick the little wastebasket and it rocketed across the room.

That bitch! How in the hell did she know about—damn it!

His cell phone vibrated on the table.

"Benjamin Graham speaking," he said curtly.

"Mr. Graham, this is Elizabeth," said a timid voice.

A wave of nausea flooded over his body. He sat down on the edge on the unmade bed. "What's going on, Liz? Everything okay at the office?"

"Oh, yes sir, everything's fine. I called to connect you to your daughter; she's waiting on the other line."

Benjamin sat up straight. "Thanks, Liz. Put her through." After a series of clicks, they were connected.

"Hello? Dad, you there?" Pam's voice said.

"Pam! What happened? You were supposed to—"

Pamela cut him off. "Hold on. Before you start going off on why I didn't fly to DC, I have something more pressing to talk to you about."

"I wasn't about to *go off*, Pamela. That's the last thing I'm in the mood for right now."

"Are you okay?" Pam's voice had softened with concern. "You don't sound too good. Have you been taking your medication?"

He pulled one of his carry-on bags toward him and rifled through the front compartment in search of the plastic pill container. It was the third time this week that he had forgotten to take his medicine, but he wasn't about to tell Pam.

"Like clockwork. Haven't missed a dose yet," he said. "I just think I may have had a little too much of the ol' rotgut last night. I'll be fine. What'd you want to talk about?"

He listened closely as Pam related the story about the Asian investors, and what they said would happen to the unnamed candidate should he win. The story made him momentarily forget about how horrific his body felt. He was stunned into silence by the time she finished.

"I'll be damned," he said at last.

"It's crazy, right?" Pam said. "Surely they couldn't be serious . . ."

"I don't know about that, sweetie," he said quietly. "There's a lot riding on this election. More than you or I could even imagine. Power shifts like that tend to make a lot of people nervous—especially powerful people. When that happens, you can bet they react—and most of the time overreact."

"So if Wynn gets elected, that will what? Put China out of business? I wouldn't think so."

"Oh, you'd better think so. Donald Wynn's position on China isn't just an act. He's been singing that song for years, and getting into a position to do something about it is right up his alley. He'll put them in a vice grip like they've never seen, and they know it." He paused. "I'll tell you what. I'm going to spread the word that Wynn may be a target. They'll clamp down on security and he should be okay. I'm staying at the Renaissance Washington right across from the convention center. Next week is the big rally, and I'm scheduled to have dinner with Wynn and his staff the night before. If I can't get the word out before then, I'll tell him myself."

"Okay, Daddy. This is all just so strange." She heaved a heavy sigh.

"Something else on your mind?"

"No, just that. Listen, I'm gonna get going. Alex and I are gonna do some catching up before I head to Beijing."

"Be sure to give me a call when you make it there. And don't worry about this. I'll handle it, okay?"

Pamela was more subdued than usual; her father knew something else was on her mind.

"You sure you don't have anything else to tell me?" he asked.

"Oh yeah, positive," she replied, far too quickly.

He knew her well enough to know she wouldn't give it up, no matter how hard he pressed. *Hell, if Catherine knows about my dealings with A. J., could Pamela know too?*

He prayed it wasn't true. She'd never understand. To this day, he wasn't positive he fully understood himself.

"Okay, sweetie. Tell Alex I said hello. I'll talk to you soon."

CHAPTER 22

In the moments after she hung up, Pamela wondered if she'd done the right thing. She wanted desperately to tell her dad about the visit from the CIA, but she just couldn't do it. She couldn't tell him Alex was a suspect, especially when she had no clue what it even was.

If only she'd told him that she knew about his membership in the Bonham Grove, telling him about the CIA's visit may have been easier. But if she hadn't confessed her knowledge of his association with the Grove by now, she more than likely never would. And what good would it have done, anyway? He would either deny it or downplay its true purpose. Either response would only drive a thicker wedge between them. She'd come to terms with the cold facts.

As she sat in the living room of the hotel suite in Madrid, she heard murmurs from Alex's room. Alex had retreated there about half an hour ago for a nap, saying the meeting had worn him out. *Is he talking in his sleep?* Pam wondered. She slipped off her heels and tiptoed to the door. The dark wood of the door was cold against her ear.

"Come on, Li, you're not making any sense," she heard Alex whisper. "Why can't you tell me? If it's that serious, just don't do it." A pause. "Okay, how about I come and help you with whatever it is?" Another pause. "No, I'm with Pam . . . Of course not. You know I wouldn't say anything."

Alex lowered his voice, and Pam could only make out a few words—
DC, last trip, Wynn. As Alex grew more frustrated, the words became a
little clearer.

"Okay, Li, this is what we'll—"

The ringing of the hotel phone made Pam jump, and her elbow
thumped against the door. Inside, Alex abruptly cut off his words. Pam
rushed to the phone, praying he hadn't heard her elbow. As she picked up
the receiver, Alex opened the door. One arm remained behind his back.

"Hello?" Pam answered, doing her best to sound casual.

It was just a woman from the front desk. Alex waved at Pam and
pointed to himself.

"One second," Pam said into the phone. Her hand covered the receiver.
"No, hon, it's just the front desk. Did it wake you up?"

Alex stretched, still keeping his right hand out of view. "Yeah, but I
needed to get up anyway."

When he disappeared back into the room, Pamela let out a breath.
He hadn't caught her listening at the door, but why had he pretended to
be asleep?

"Sorry about that," Pam said, resuming the phone conversation. "I'm
here now."

"No problem, ma'am. We were just calling you to let you know that a
package for you just arrived. Shall I have it sent up?"

Pam thought about it. The package from Formula One would contain
the itinerary for her Beijing assignment. She'd left Roxy a message and
asked her to overnight it to the hotel.

"No thanks, I'll come and get it later," said Pam. "There's no rush."

Pam hung up and dialed Formula One's main office in Switzerland.

"Formula One, this is Helen, may I help you?"

Pam hesitated and lowered the phone. *Should I do this?*

"Hello? Hello? Is anyone there?" Helen asked.

Pamela moved her finger over the red button to end the call, then
paused. Instead of disconnecting she pulled the phone back to her face.

"Hey, Helen, it's Pamela Graham. Listen, I've had a family emergency.
Could you check the schedules and find out if anyone can cover for me in
Beijing? I really don't think I can make it."

"Oh sure, Pam. I'll see what we can do and get back to you. Is every-thing okay?"

"Yeah, everything's fine. Well, maybe not *fine*, but I'll be able to work it out."

Helen was silent on the other end of the line, perhaps waiting for Pam to fill in details. This was a big assignment she was skipping, but Pam chose to leave it at that.

Helen sighed before she spoke. "No worries, dear. I'll bet Rodney can fill in for you in Beijing. But if you need to talk to someone, you know I'm—"

"I know, Helen, and thank you," Pam said.

Pam hung up quickly and contemplated her next move. She lowered her head, trying to will an answer from thin air. Nothing. She sat there for several more minutes, plans racing through her mind. Her trance was bro-ken when Alex walked in.

"You okay?" he asked. Concern filled his eyes.

"Oh, I'm fine, hon," Pam smiled.

Alex twisted his lower lip but didn't press her. "So you're not going to Beijing?"

Pam hesitated but decided there was no need to lie.

"Yeah, something came up. I need to meet up with my dad in DC," she said.

"I want to come with you." Alex paused. "I mean, is that okay?"

Pam paused. He knew that he was always welcome. Did he ask this because he knew this wasn't a normal situation? She didn't want to think about the possibility. The CIA agent had mentioned his name . . . and he'd been so friendly with the Asian investors, who, moments before, had been casually discussing an assassination.

"Why would you think otherwise, Alex?" she asked.

Alex shrugged. "I don't know. You just seem a little . . . distracted lately. But I could be wrong."

"You don't miss a beat, do ya? There is a lot of stuff on my mind, but you know me—I'll be okay."

Alex gave her a half-smile. "All right, if you say so. Guess I better start getting my things together."

"You do that. And don't worry about me. I'll be fine. I'm gonna head down and check us out, but I'll be right back."

He walked into his bedroom, head down. Pam listened as he unzipped his bag and threw in piles of clothing.

Seems like there's a lot on your mind too, kiddo.

CHAPTER 23

As the glass elevator descended to the lobby, Benjamin Graham peered out over the hotel's interior. The slow, even descent gave him time to ponder where his life had ended up. Things were falling apart faster and faster, and he couldn't seem to get everything back in one piece.

Just before the elevator reached the lobby, he spotted Catherine's silver bob. She was back at the bar, again surrounded by a small group of people.

"Ain't that a kick in the jock strap," he mumbled.

He stepped into the lobby and moved along the wall farthest from the bar, doing his best to stay out of sight of Catherine's group. He slipped into a lounge area and sat in an armchair next to a four-foot dividing wall.

Over the wall, he had a clear view of Catherine's group. Standing just a few feet from his nemesis was a slender Asian youth with a familiar face. *I know that kid*, he thought.

A flash of recognition in his mind. A year before—Pamela had just gotten back from a trip to Rhode Island. She was at the office going on and on about Alexander's early graduation from Brown. That day, she'd given him a wallet-sized photo, one of many she took at the event.

"*He looked so handsome in his cap and gown,*" Pam had said, beaming at the photo. "*Oh, and this is his best bud, Li. If I had a dollar for every time I had to get those two out of trouble!*"

Benjamin dug one elbow into his armrest, lifted his body, and reached into his back pocket for his wallet. Stuffed into a thick wad of business cards was the same photo. Benjamin was ashamed to realize he'd only looked at it a few times since it was given to him, but now that he had it in front of him, there was no mistaking it: The Asian youth across the lobby was also the person in the photo, standing next to Alex in the bright sunlight.

"*His best bud, Li,*" Pam had said. He'd heard about Li periodically from Pam—there was always a story of his and Alex's shenanigans. Now this Li character was hobnobbing with Catherine Caddaric.

He watched, almost refusing to blink, as Catherine patted Li on the shoulder lightly and moved away, whispering something in the ear of a fierce-looking Asian woman.

If this isn't the strangest shit I've ever seen, I don't know what is.

Benjamin sunk in his seat, now completely shielded by the wall. He pulled out his cell phone and snapped a picture of the group at the bar before dialing his office.

"Liz, it's me. Get Pamela on the line as fast as you can."

"I'll try, sir, but she called in from out of the country," said Elizabeth.

"China already?"

"No, not China. It was a collect call from Spain."

"Spain? All right. Stay close to your phone. I may be calling you right back."

Benjamin stood, checked his path, and walked toward the main set of elevators across the lobby. A bellhop stood before the doors with a cart of luggage. The up arrow was illuminated.

When the doors slid open, Benjamin allowed the bellhop to enter, then slipped in behind him.

"Hey, hon, I'm on my way up," he said into the dead phone. "I'm just giving a tip to the young man who brought up our breakfast." He pulled out a fifty-dollar bill as he spoke and passed it to the bellhop.

The worker's eyes expanded. He pointed at himself in confusion.

"Okay . . . Okay," Ben said. "See you in a bit . . . Oh, hon? Be sure to unlock the door. I left my key in the . . . Huh? Hon?"

He looked over at the bellhop, who was still hypnotized by the bill in his hand.

"Guess she got cut off," said Ben, slipping the phone back into his pocket. The elevator was still; neither of them had pressed a button.

The worker pulled in his lips. "Uh, sir? I don't think this was meant for me. I just started my shift ten minutes ago."

"What? I thought for sure it was you who brought up that delicious breakfast."

The bellhop bit his lower lip and, after a moment's thought, held the bill out toward Benjamin.

"Hold on now—what are you trying to do, get me yelled at by the missus? Listen, she's on this tip kick lately, so she had me come down here and hunt for the guy who brought us breakfast. She was pissed, said I stiffed him. It's our anniversary, so I was just trying to keep her happy and . . ." Benjamin snapped his fingers. "Hey, kid, I have an idea." He pointed to the luggage rack. "Where are you taking this stuff?"

"To the third floor, sir," he said.

"Well, my wallet's in my room. How about you follow me up there and I'll give you another fifty to fetch me some roses for her this evening."

The worker's eyes lit up. "Sure, sir! I can do that. No problem!"

Benjamin pressed the button for the top floor, but it didn't light up.

"Here you are, sir!" The worker slipped his card into a slot in the elevator's wall. "You have to use your key to get access to the top floors."

"Oh, right. I hate trying to keep up with all those key cards. I usually let the missus hold on to all of them, but then this happens—you get stuck in the lobby. Still better this way, though. If they get lost, I won't be the one who gets chewed out—know what I mean?"

The bellhop laughed.

On the top floor, Benjamin led the bellhop directly to Catherine's room and immediately rapped on the door. It was a gamble, but not a very risky one—she was in the bar. He just hoped she didn't have an assistant in there.

"Cathy, honey, it's me!" he shouted into the door, continuing to knock. "I left my key in your purse. Can you open the door!"

Nothing. After a few more seconds, Benjamin placed his ear to the door.

"Ahhhh, I can hear the shower running."

The worker sprung into action. "Here you are, sir! Let me get it!" He pushed his access key into the slot and unlocked the door.

Benjamin stepped into the dark apartment, allowing the door to partially close behind him. Out of the bellhop's sight, he waited for a minute, then pulled his wallet out of his jacket. He opened the door and passed the worker another fifty.

"Hey, kid, here you are. Just keep the money and have a good one, okay? Forget the flowers."

The worker stared at the prize in his hand, incredulous. "Really? Thank you so much, sir! If you need anything at all, just ask for Vincent."

Benjamin closed the door, alone in the suite—he hoped. He switched on a lamp and swept the room with his eyes, searching for clues to what she was up to. The place was immaculate. He opened drawer after drawer only to find neatly folded clothing.

He moved to the desk, where a pad of stationery sat, the palm tree logo printed on each page. He thumbed through the sheets of paper—all blank. He moved on to the open laptop next to the pad and tapped the spacebar. The computer hummed to life. In front of him was the last document Catherine had been looking at.

He immediately recognized it as a portfolio. He leaned in, scrutinizing the long list of stocks, bonds, and mutual funds.

As he looked, it started to all come together—why Catherine was in DC, her connection with Li, her sudden interest in the election. What had once seemed illogical was starting to look like sinister brilliance.

CHAPTER 24

Pam stood with Alex on the sidewalk outside the Eurostars Madrid Tower, digging through her purse.

"Alex, honey, I think I left my planner in the room. I'm gonna run up and get it, but I'll be *right* back."

"You'd better not leave me waiting here forever," Alex said with grin.

Pamela shot him a look of mock sternness as she turned on her heel. *Always forgetting something.*

She clicked across the lobby in her heels and pressed the gold-plated button to call down one of the three elevators. Right away, the mirrored doors chimed and spread apart, presenting a massive interior. Even after riding it several times, she marveled at the sheer size of the elevator. She stepped on and pressed "12."

Just before the doors closed, they stopped and reversed direction, revealing a tall Asian man.

He lowered his head and boarded the elevator. Though he now wore thick-rimmed glasses, she was almost sure it was him—the investor who'd been so eager to tell his Russian friend about China's contingency plan should Wynn be elected.

The man now stood behind her, far too close for the size of the eleva-tor. She pressed the button for the twelfth floor again. As the doors slid together, the man reached forward and brushed against Pamela as he pressed the button for thirteen.

Pam clutched her bag tighter as they rose. She remained facing forward, but in the mirrored wall she could see him. His gaze was fixed on the floor.

Ding!

The elevator slowed as it reached the third floor. *Someone else is getting on!* Pam thought. *Thank God!*

The doors opened to reveal another somber-looking Asian man. Pamela's skin tingled as she watched him join the other man at the rear of the elevator and lock his hands in front of him. Even behind a convincing fake goatee, there was no mistaking the shorter investor from the meeting.

Oh my God. She could hardly move.

As the doors closed once again, both of the men unlocked their hands in front of them and unbuttoned their jackets. She saw the shorter of them lower his right hand to his side before he spread his fingers wide, extending and retracting them twice. She read the body language easily: He was getting ready to draw a weapon.

At the last possible second she stuck the toe of her shoe into the narrowing gap between the doors. The doors reversed direction, and she swiftly slipped through the crack. In the hall, she broke into a sprint. Seconds later, she'd made it to the end of the hall. She shoved open the heavy metal door and darted up the stairwell two steps at a time.

Before she made it up one flight, she heard the heavy stairwell door slam against the wall. They were after her.

She pushed her body with everything she had. The air of the stairwell was hot and thick; she felt like she was inhaling dirt. Below her, the pounding footsteps seemed to be catching up. She had no idea how far these men were willing to go to keep her silent. If they caught her, would she be able to convince them she hadn't heard a thing?

Halfway up the eighth floor, her legs began to quiver from exhaustion, and she questioned the wisdom of running upstairs rather than down. The leather lining of her shoes dug into the top of her feet. She could ignore the pain, but she couldn't press on much longer without passing out. On the next floor, she was going to have to make a break out of the stairwell.

Pamela burst through the door that led to the ninth floor, ran past the elevators, and careened to the right, down a carpeted hallway. A gold-plated sign displayed an arrow and numbers; she was headed toward rooms 900 through 950. She tore down the empty corridor, the end seeming to recede farther and farther the faster she ran.

Bam! She heard the stairwell door fly open and slam into the wall. She'd hoped that somehow they'd keep running up, but it hadn't worked. She didn't want to look back, but she had to see how close they were. When she whipped her head around, still running, she saw that both men had rounded the corner, the shorter one taking the lead.

At the end of the hall, an exit sign glowed in bright red. Just a few more feet and she would arrive at another set of stairs. *Down this time, Pamela. Down!*

She dove for the door, jerking hard on the handle. The door stayed in place. *Locked.* Her options had dwindled to zero.

She kicked the door hard. Her shoe clanged against the metal with no effect.

Damn it!

With her next kick, the door swung open. Before she could even run into the dark stairwell, a hand reached out, grabbed her arm, and pulled her in.

CHAPTER 25

" Shhh!"

The man released her arm and secured a thick iron bar across the door handles. It didn't look like much of a barricade to Pam, but right now she was grateful for any help she could get. In the dark of the stairwell, she recognized the pointed chin and shifty eyes of Steven, the first presenter from the meeting.

He pointed up. "Can't talk now. We have to get up to the next floor."

Pam was amazed to see the blundering speaker now delivering lines like an action hero.

The pounding of the men's fists on the other side of the door reverberated in the stairwell. Pam and Steven dashed up a flight and onto the tenth floor. Motioning for her to follow, he bounded down the hallway. He stopped about three-fourths of the way, panting for breath, and pulled out a key card. With a click and a green flash from the lock, he pushed inside, Pamela rushing in after him.

Steven turned the dead bolt, pushed a plush armchair in front of the door, and ran across the room to pull the thick beige curtains tightly closed.

Pamela leaned over a table, pulling in deep breaths, a hand to her chest. "Where did you come from? You . . . you work for Mazarredo, right?"

"In addition to some other, less-than-reputable organizations," he replied, "but we'll get into that later." He stalked back to the door and put his eye to the peephole. "I saw the Bin boys on the prowl for you and figured I'd rush up to meet you at your room. Got lucky and found you in the stairwell—seemingly just in time."

"What on earth is going on here? I'm confused as hell right about now."

"Believe me, at first I was just as confused as you." He now placed an ear to the door. "They came to you just like they came to me."

"Those guys?" Pam asked.

He turned to her quickly. "The damn CIA!"

Pam looked at him blankly. *But those weren't CIA agents after me. They were investors at the company you work for!*

"I know they talked to you. Same bastards came to me about a month ago. I was in Oklahoma on business when I get this knock on the door. They marched right in, started going off about someone I know being in bed with the enemy. Hate to say it, but they kind of implied it was someone at Mazarredo." He peeked out the curtains again. "They said they wanted me to do some *observation* for them. Can you believe it? Like I'm some dumbass who doesn't know what that means. It was pretty damn clear they wanted me to spy on the very people I work for. I know no Mazarredo would get tied up in what they're talking about—not Jorge, not Alex, not anyone."

He moved away from the window and began pacing. He pulled a pack of Marlboros from his pocket, popped one out into his palm, and placed it in his mouth, working the unlit cigarette with his lips.

Pam stood in silence. Questions filled her mind, but she wanted all this guy's information before she said a word.

He pulled the cigarette out of his mouth. "Oh, I stopped smoking these things a long time ago, but putting one between my lips helps calm my nerves. Anyway, I never had any intention of telling them shit. There wasn't anything to tell as far as I knew. When the guy was still in my room, he got a call; he took away my phone and shut me up in the bathroom while he took it. Guess he didn't realize how thin those walls were, 'cause I heard a lot of what he said. Something about talking to 'his mother in Dallas.' So when Alex told me you were in town, I didn't say anything, but I did put two and two together."

He stopped and looked at Pam. "Actually, you don't look anything like I imagined. You're damn near a legend around here, you know? Jorge told us all about how you got Alex out of Russia."

If only they knew the rest of that story, thought Pamela. *Getting out of Russia was just the beginning.*

"No one, at least not me, ever expected to actually meet you," Steven continued. "Jorge never told us your name, so a lot of us thought it was just a fanciful story, something to make his beloved Alex seem larger than life."

Pam stood. "Sorry, this is just a lot to take in. The only thing I can focus on right now is the fact that I was just chased through a hotel—probably by men who want to kill me. Those weren't CIA, Steven. They're after me for something else entirely. After the meeting yesterday, I heard—"

"Oh, I know about that, too. But I wouldn't say they're disconnected. The Bin boys are livid about what you heard. Those two are relatives of President Bin, maybe even his own brothers, but don't quote me on that. I heard them talking in Mandarin at the bar about how you overheard them—they had no idea you spoke English. Seems like a pretty bad oversight to me, but then they didn't suspect that I spoke Mandarin either."

He stared at her again. "You know, I expected you to look more like a female boxer from the stories about all the ass-kicking you did. You do remind me of your dad, though."

"My dad?" *Who the hell is this guy?* Her mind reeled at his knowledge of so many parts of her life.

"Yeah—Benjamin Graham? My uncle thinks the world of him, just like everyone else."

Pam folded her arms. "Is that right? I'd say my dad has plenty of people who dislike him. Probably even a skeleton or two in the closet."

Steven lifted his pointed chin. "Is that right? My opinion—not that you asked—is that he's one hell of a man. What he's doing takes more guts than most people have, although I suppose not too many people know about that side of him."

"A lot of people run publishing companies, Steven," she said. "And what do you mean? That side?"

"Good lord, I'm not talking about publishing. I'm talking about—you know, the whole undercover thing."

Steven listened at the door, the unlit cigarette extended between two fingers as if it were actually lit. Satisfied that no one was on the other side of the door, he walked back to the window and peeked out at the street below. "I know that I sure as hell wouldn't have done it."

Pam sat on the arm of the sofa. "Look, Steven, you're gonna have to fill me in. I'm lost as hell."

He stopped pacing and turned to her. "You serious?"

"Very," Pam said.

Steven threw his hands in the air. "That is unbelievable! You're telling me Benjamin Graham kept that even from you? Wow. Listen, if you weren't his daughter, there's no way in hell I'd tell you this, but I'm sure you'd have found out sooner or later."

CHAPTER 26

A lex stood outside the hotel's entrance, next to a pile of luggage. He glanced at his watch as another taxi pulled up. Just like the previous two, he waved it off. He turned back to the building, trying to catch a glimpse of Pam through the dark glass. Still no sign of her. She'd been gone for nearly twenty minutes.

He'd noticed the Bin brothers disappear into the lobby just after Pam, but hadn't thought much of it. Now, Pam's long absence had begun to worry him. He'd had that strange conversation with Li, and Pam had seemed uneasy since the meeting.

Alex pulled one of the parking attendants aside. He had wavy brown hair and an open face.

The young man gave Alex a little bow. "Mr. Mazarredo. How can I help you?"

"Keep an eye on my bags?" He passed the attendant a twenty-euro bill. "I'll be right back." Alex took a step toward the entrance, then turned back. "And could you do me another favor?"

"Yes sir?"

"I'm only twenty—could you just call me Alex?"

The attendant laughed. *"No problemo!"*

* * *

Pamela sat perched on the arm of the couch in Steven's room, waiting for him to drop the big reveal about her father.

"What have you got? I'm pretty sure I know more about my dad than you think I do."

Steven tapped a thin finger against his chin. He hesitated, then nodded to himself as if he'd come to a decision.

"My uncle is Alvin James."

Pam's expression was blank.

"Alvin James—code name A. J. The guy who infiltrated the Bonham Grove," Steven explained.

Pam's eyes widened. "Oh, okay, I'm with you now. I've definitely heard of him. But what's he got to do—"

"He was the one who asked your dad to do it."

"Do what?"

"How could you not know? He convinced your dad to pretend that he wanted to be a member of the Grove! They met before my uncle made a name for himself by exposing the secret workings of the Grove. Before him, it was all guesswork, but now we know all about what goes on when the most powerful men in the world get together each year in California. In between the boozing and rituals, they map out the new world order. The mainstream press still won't pick it up, but those of us paying attention owe your dad and my uncle a lot.

"It just so happens that on the day that your dad received an invitation to join the Grove, he got a call from my uncle. Ben told him about the invitation and laughed about it—your dad had no interest in joining. A few months later, when Uncle Al was figuring out how to uncover their actions, he gave your dad a call. Your dad ended up accepting and helping my uncle. They're the only two who have successfully snuck in and brought the Grove's activities to the outside world."

Pam cupped her face in her hands. "I don't believe it."

"Yeah, brass balls. Like I said, I sure as hell wouldn't have done it. You know what will happen if they find out your dad was just there to feed information to my uncle? You're damn right: He'll be holding hands with Hoffa, that's wha—" Steven stopped. "Shit, I'm sorry Pam."

"Don't worry about it," Pam said. "I'm—I'm still in shock here."

A hasty knock sounded on the door of the hotel room. Steven snapped to attention. His wide eyes locked on the doorknob as if he were expecting a visit from the grim reaper.

"Listen, you'd better hide somewhere," he said shakily. His eyes searched the room for a place to conceal her. "That has to be the Bin brothers, or worse. I . . . have no idea how they found me."

Pam ran into the bedroom and dashed behind the bar that stood in the corner. More hard knocks. Apparently Steven didn't plan to answer.

The crash of the door's lock giving way resounded through the room. Words in a language that sounded a lot like Mandarin were shouted.

Then Pam heard a familiar voice—Steven. "Okay, okay. But tell them to put those things away!"

"Where's the woman?" said a heavily accented voice.

"What woman?"

There was a heavy thud, followed by a sharp smack.

"Search the room!" the same voice ordered.

The bedroom door swung opened. Pam curled her body into the smallest ball possible as someone entered. She heard steps toward the adjoined bathroom and the shower curtains being jerked to one side. More doors were opened and then slammed.

Another thud shook the floor. It sounded like someone had dropped a set of hundred-pound weights. Seconds later, there was a heavy grunt.

"Hey! What was that?" the person in the bathroom shouted.

Pam tried to turn her head as slowly as possible to see if he was headed toward her.

A wide shadow fell over her. She looked up to find the shorter Asian man from the elevator leaning over the bar and looking down at her. He pulled his coat to the side, reached in his jacket, and pulled out a short, black pistol.

He didn't say a word as he continued to look down on her with dark, merciless eyes. He lowered the gun until it was pointed directly at her head.

Pamela closed her eyes. *This is it.*

Nothing. Then a sound like a bat hitting raw meat.

Pam opened her eyes and rolled away just before the entire bar toppled over, crashing to the floor right where she'd been hiding. The Asian man lay sprawled on the floor, the gun tossed several feet from his hand. Blood trickled from his right temple and onto the carpet.

Standing over him with an iron rod still gripped tightly in his hand was Alex. His chest heaved with heavy breaths as he looked down at the man he had just smashed in the head.

CHAPTER 27

Twenty-six hours remained before the massive Wynn rally would begin. Gas prices were so high that abandoned cars on the side of the road were now a common sight. The stock market teetered on the edge of a major crash while the US debt peaked. Other countries had begun to question America's ability to bounce back.

Benjamin sat in front of his computer, a glass of scotch in his hand. He was scrolling through a website that listed public information on companies in China as well as their major shareholders. It was no surprise to see one name surface again and again. Everything aligned perfectly with what he'd seen in Catherine's portfolio.

He switched to another page that displayed the Chinese government's recent investments. They were concentrating their money in what looked like a strategic effort to affect both European and American markets.

There's the smoke. Now let's find that fire.

Using keywords like *China, investments, manufacturing, United States,* and *oil,* he pulled up article after article. His eyes darted back and forth as he soaked up the information like a sponge. When he stumbled across an article from the previous day's *Wall Street Journal,* he slowed his pace to take in every word.

The title of the article was "China's Silent War," and it tracked how China was quietly selling off billions of US dollars it had in reserves for investments in precious metals, oil, and the Japanese yen. The move was systematically decreasing the value of the US dollar. Soon, it was likely to lose its place as the global reserve currency.

Catherine, you are one sadistic bitch.

He downed the entire glass of scotch, poured himself another, and downed it. He made several calls, trying to confirm the dinner with Wynn he was supposed to attend that night. No one was returning his calls, and the time and location hadn't been set.

On the sidewalk below, he saw carefree people bustling along. As much as he wanted to get out of the room, he decided to order from the menu. He ate a hefty portion of lasagna and guzzled three more scotches as he pored over the articles, websites, and stock figures. After a couple of hours, he sat back in his chair and rubbed his eyes.

"And there's the fire," he said aloud. "And it's one hell of an inferno."

CHAPTER 28

Catherine smiled as she placed the receiver back on the hook and casu-ally made her way across the hotel room. A muscle-bound Asian woman sat slumped in a chair, lost in her own thoughts.

"Just got off the line with President Bin, Zhao," Catherine said. "He seems to think it would be better if we got a freelancer to take care of this."

Zhao tightened her jaw and began tapping a pen against the tabletop. "Why he make a change? He think I cannot do it?"

Catherine paced a hand on Zhao's shoulder. "Relax, dear. I'm sure it's nothing like that. I think he just wants to make sure that this doesn't get linked back to him." Catherine looked at her watch. "Where's Li?"

Zhao hunched her shoulders moodily. "Guess he stepped out."

"What does he think about all of this? Does he understand how impor-tant it is for us to keep things as they are?"

Zhao scratched her forehead. "I guess. I know he father toll him. That is all that matter. He do anything for he father. He own idea do not matter. It is the way we do."

"Good." Catherine's smile faded as she noticed Zhao's diminished enthusiasm. "Zhao, are you okay? You seem . . . different."

Zhao sat up and placed her wide forearms on the table. She stared blankly across the room for a moment, then lifted her head. "Just thought I here to do more."

"Oh, but you are," said Catherine. "I know who I'm going to call to take care of this Wynn issue, but there are going to be a lot of people trying to stop him—even if they have absolutely no chance of pulling it off. But for the ones that try, I want you to do whatever you feel is necessary to keep them out of his way."

Zhao cracked her knuckles, leaned back in her chair, and crossed her mannish arms. A hint of a smile flickered across her chiseled face. "This I can do."

Catherine gave her another pat on the shoulder and pulled out her phone. The number she needed to call was locked into her memory, though it had been some time since she used it. She certainly couldn't write it down.

Catherine dialed the number and waited.

The process was always the same. She simply had to hang up after three rings. No more than ten minutes later, she would get a call from an unlisted number.

This time, the return call came within a few seconds.

"Hello?" she answered.

"Location?" a monotone voice asked.

"Wallace Convention Center: 801 Mount Vernon."

"Time?"

"Tomorrow, between seven and eight p.m., Eastern time."

"How many guests?"

"One," said Catherine.

"Name and deposit by midnight." The line went dead.

Catherine went straight to the computer and electronically wired $50,000 to the account. The other $50,000 would be sent after the job was completed.

The final step was to log into a fake pest-control website. She clicked the contact page and typed in a few lines. In the comment section, she entered "Donald Wynn."

She clicked Send.

Zhao's eyes were trained on Catherine from across the room.

"This person good?"

"I'd say so." Catherine walked over to the bar and poured herself a glass of wine, filling it almost to the rim.

"He a sniper?"

"Something like that. He's a Navy Seal—or at least he used to be—but that's all I know. I met him only once. Since then, we only communicate this way."

Zhao nodded but looked unconvinced. "I hear Navy Seals very good. They get to Bin Laden, right?"

Catherine laughed lightly as she walked over to the window. "Well, that compound raid was a good piece of PR, at least."

"So he still alive?" asked Zhao.

"No, he's dead all right. Just not from us. Did you notice the cane he walked with, and the long arms? Marfan syndrome. He could've lived a normal life with treatment, but when he was forced to go into hiding, he declined rapidly. He was gone by late '02."

Zhao gaped at her. "You kidding . . ."

"Not at all. See, his death was the ace in the hole they used to put the general public at ease. The country was going through a hard time, so they flicked the stage lights and that was that. They orchestrated a raid, pretended they got him, and let the rejoicing begin. A short time after the raid, those same Navy Seals were involved in a fatal accident so that they could never reveal the truth."

"That crazy," Zhao said.

"Like a fox, my dear," Catherine said with a smile.

CHAPTER 29

Pam and Alex stepped out of the taxi in front of the Renaissance Washington Hotel, exhausted. The flight from Madrid had been long and full of uneasiness. Flashbacks plagued her—blood flowing from the Asian investor's head; Steven's body slumped lifeless on the floor. She'd been distraught there in Steven's room, but Alex, amazingly, had kept a cool head. He listened to her story about the accidental eavesdropping without emotion, but he said they had all the more reason to get to DC as soon as possible. He'd examined Steven's body and found that he was badly pistol whipped but still breathing.

As for the two Asian men, Pam had no idea whether they awoke from their injuries. Alex had delivered one heavy blow to the back of each of their heads. They'd carried Steven downstairs and called for help, but left immediately. They couldn't afford to get entangled in the situation. Pam had no idea how Alex would tell his father he'd knocked two potential Mazarredo investors out cold, but he didn't seem concerned about it. The two of them were silent for most of the flight over the Atlantic, choosing to ruminate rather than discuss.

To add to her agitation, she'd discovered six missed calls when she turned on her cell phone after the flight, each from an unlisted number. No messages had been left. She had a feeling she knew who that was, but she wasn't about to tell them anything.

"You okay?" Alex asked. Pamela had paused and gripped her thigh on the sidewalk outside the Renaissance Washington.

"Think so," she replied. "Just pulled something, probably, but I'm sure it'll work itself out."

"Might be that O-L-D creeping up on ya," Alex joked.

The first bit of light banter since the attack in Madrid lightened Pam's spirits, and she playfully swung her bag at Alex. He nimbly jumped to the side but almost lost his balance. Pam lunged after him and grabbed his arm just before he fell backward.

"Okay, kiddo, no more goofing off. We've got serious work to do."

Alex's face turned grave again. She could see that he knew just how serious it was.

* * *

Benjamin stood in front of the closet mirror, rubbing his hand across the rough stubble that had sprouted from his face. The phone was on its fifth ring, but he remained in a trance, his mind sorting through possibilities, options, strategies. After six or seven more rings, he shook himself to awareness and walked over to the nightstand.

"Benjamin Graham speaking."

"Hello, Mr. Graham," the desk clerk said cheerily. "We have someone here at the desk who's trying to contact you. Hold on one moment, please."

"Thanks," he said.

A second later, he heard his daughter's voice. "Dad? It's me."

"Pam? You're here? In Washington? I thought for sure you'd be in Beijing by now."

"No, Dad. Big change of plans. I'm in the lobby with Alex. They wouldn't give me your room number and you weren't answering your cell, so I had to have them call you."

Benjamin smiled for the first time in days. "I'm in 903. Come on up!"

CHAPTER 30

L i lifted his head just in time to spot Alex and Pamela walking through the lobby of the Renaissance Washington. Had he looked up a moment later, he would've missed them entirely. He coughed to avoid choking on his bourbon and set his sweating tumbler down on the reflective tabletop.

Immediately Li replayed the last conversation he'd had with Alex and their bitter argument about Li's father. The confrontation was still fresh in his head. As far as he was concerned, a sacred line had been crossed. He couldn't forgive Alex for questioning the way his father ran his country. Only because it was Alex had Li walked away and let the matter drop.

Did I tell him too much? Li wracked his brain but couldn't come up with any rational reason for why Alex was here, now.

Li slumped down in his seat, shielding himself from view. His eyes followed Pam and Alex as they moved toward the front desk. He gulped down some more bourbon, watching them over the rim of his glass as they disappeared around the corner. *I hope for your sake that you guys aren't here to try to stop this.*

He set down the glass and pulled his cell phone from his pocket.

"Hello?" she answered.

"Hey, Catherine. It's Li."

"Li, we were just talking about you," Catherine said brightly. "What did you do, sneak away? Were we boring you, dear?"

"No, not at all. Just came down for a drink."

"Well now, there's certainly nothing wrong with that. But you do know you could've helped yourself to something from the minibar, right?"

Li ran his finger along the mouth of the tumbler. "Yeah, I know, but the overpriced drinks at the bar just taste better to me."

Catherine laughed. "Between you and me, I feel the same way."

"So, do we have a game plan for tonight?"

"Funny you should ask. I just finished talking to your father. He is very pleased with our plan, but he wants you to get back to Beijing right away. The next flight doesn't leave till nine-thirty, so you'll be able to see most of the rally and still make it to the airport in plenty of time. My driver will be outside the hotel waiting for you just after eight."

"Thanks, Catherine." He hung up, trying not to be angry at how she followed his father's orders like that—without even consulting him.

Li tapped his phone back to life and dialed another number.

"Hello?" answered a throaty female voice.

"Zhao, I need to talk to you."

"Yes," she said.

Li sat up in his seat. "Don't say anything to Catherine, but Alex and his mother just walked into the hotel."

"Alex? You friend?"

"Yes, him. I told him I was coming here, but I didn't tell him why. I . . . I hope he didn't figure it out."

"What you say to him?"

"Nothing significant."

"Then why he here?"

"I'm not sure. Back in Spain, he started asking me a lot of questions about our country and the way my father was running it. So I left early to come here."

"I would kill him," Zhao said flatly.

"I know you would've, but—"

"But? He dishonor your father. There only one solution."

Li was silent.

"Again," Zhao continued, "why he here now?"

"I have no idea, Zhao! He called me after I left Spain. I told him I needed to do something in DC, but I didn't say what."

"If he get in my way, I take care of him. And if you let he get in your way, I tell your father."

"Yes, I know. But that will not happen."

"You father knew you let friend disrespect him, he very disappointed."

"You're right, Zhao."

"I know."

Li could always count on Zhao for an unwavering opinion. She was a straight shooter who knew how to look past the means and remain focused on the end. As he'd expected, their short talk had realigned Li's priorities.

He was the only son of the president of China, and his position came with nonnegotiable requirements. Perhaps if he and Alex had talked more about politics and less about girls in college, his friend would have understood that concept.

I don't know why you're here, but you should have remained in Spain, my friend.

CHAPTER 31

"This is Alex?" Benjamin bellowed. "What happened to the scrawny kid I used to know!" He grabbed Alex's arms. "Look at those guns! You've grown into quite the lady-killer, huh?"

Alex smiled broadly and embraced Benjamin in a tight bear hug. Pamela waited for the men to finish, then embraced her dad hard.

Her eyes filled with tears as he wrapped his arms around her. It felt impossible to let go of the regret building inside her. She'd misjudged him all these years, at great cost to their relationship. It was all her fault.

"Hey, sweetheart!" He pulled back and noticed the tears. "What's this all about?"

Pam wiped the moisture from her eyes. "Nothing, Dad. Just a lot on my mind and . . . ya know, glad to be back in the States."

Benjamin laid a hand tenderly on her shoulder.

"See, what did I tell ya? All that damned Formula One travel is finally wearing you down."

Pam grinned. "Okay, Dad, if you say so."

"I'm happy to see you, but as much as I hate to admit it, it might have been better if you went on to Beijing," he said. "There's a damn hell-storm brewing here in DC."

"Don't I know it," she said, taking out her phone and dialing Roxy.

Benjamin turned his attention to Alex. "I hear you're destined for big things over there at your father's company."

Alex smiled and gave a humble shrug.

"I think it's a little early to say," he said. "Just trying to step in and keep everything going like it had been. If I can just do that, I'll be happy. I'm stepping into a situation that was already up and running; my dad did all the real work."

Benjamin gave Alex a pat on the shoulder. "Now that's how ya do it. You just keep being there for your family, okay, kid? No one is gonna care about that company more than you do. Mazarredo is a part of you now— don't ever forget that."

The stern look Pam got from her father didn't surprise her. She knew whose benefit this little talk was for. She looked back at her phone, pretending to read.

"Yes sir," Alex said.

Benjamin moved to the window that overlooked the Wallace Convention Center. A congested Ninth Street flowed with endless traffic.

"Guys, it's a crazy-ass world out there," he said as he watched the mob below. "And I'm telling you now, it ain't gonna get sane anytime soon."

Pamela turned off her cell phone. It was the fourth time she'd tried Roxy to no avail. "Dad, did you ever get in touch with Wynn's people about . . . you know?"

"I was scheduled to have dinner with them, but I never heard back from anyone." He stopped, distracted by the television. The volume was off, but a bold graphic showed another heavy drop for the Dow. He pointed at the screen. "Would you look at that? I guess I should've expected a cancellation; there's a hell of a lot going on out there. I'll just have to let them know tonight, at the rally."

Pamela looked at her watch. "Well, we've got plenty of time until it starts. How's the food here? I'm starved."

"It ain't Texas barbecue, I can tell you that much. But it's a stomach full," he said.

"A stomach full? That doesn't sound very appealing, Dad." She turned to Alex. He was texting furiously. "You hungry, hon?"

"No, you go ahead," he said without looking up. "Not that hungry."

"You wanna get a bite to eat, Dad?"

Benjamin glanced at his computer. "I need to get some work done, but"—he looked over at Alex—"I'll walk you to the elevators."

They stepped out into the hall together, but Benjamin stopped after a few steps and took Pam by the wrist.

"I wanted to talk to you about something, Pam," he said, rubbing his unshaven face with one hand. "Have you been keeping close contact with Alex—since he's been in Spain, I mean? Has he changed at all personality-wise?"

The vague implications the CIA agent had made during his visit flooded back into Pam's mind. And there was the whispered phone call at the hotel—the one he'd lied to her about. It was all circumstantial, but she had to admit she felt the knot of fear in her stomach harden at her father's question.

"No, Dad. Why do you ask?"

"Can't say exactly. I just . . . worry about him."

"I haven't been around him as much as the typical parent would have been around her child, but I know his heart. He is and has always been a good person."

Benjamin nodded. "I know Pam, I know. But you know how it is. Young people get influenced. The right person at the right time can muddle the old thought process." He scratched his head. "You know, it could happen to anyone. Hell, it's even happened to me."

Pam looked at her father's concerned face. It was time. "Dad . . . I know all about the Grove."

"You *what!*" he shouted. He looked up and down the empty hall before continuing in a lowered voice. "How the . . . it's not what you think."

"I know that too," she said. "Why didn't you ever tell me?"

"How . . . how did you—"

"Alvin Jones's nephew—he works for Mazarredo. It's a long story, but he told me about it, only because he knew I was your daughter. Actually, he assumed I knew and just blurted it out. No one else knows."

The color had now drained completely from Ben's face.

"Was it worth it?" Pam asked.

Benjamin angled his head, thinking about the question. "Actually no. I did it in the beginning because the company was in bad financial shape.

A. J. told me he would split the profits with me, and he did. I fed him the inside information about the club, and he exposed it."

"But he was able to get in and out. Why didn't you just do the same thing?"

Benjamin gave Pam a sad smile. "Alvin was never a member. He hacked into the Grove's computer system—and to this day, he's the only person to have crossed those guys and lived. But if a known member were to leave and be exposed as a mole"—he brought his finger to his own chest—"it's doubtful that person would live."

Pam was overwhelmed.

"After he hacked in, he got even more information from me, and every bit of it was true. I only found out that membership in the Grove is a one-way ticket after I was in. Once you're accepted, there's no getting out."

Despite the sickening feeling growing in her gut, Pam smiled weakly and tried to find a positive spin on his position. "Look, Dad, I know playing the role of a card-carrying member isn't the best thing in the world, but no one will ever know but you, me, and A. J."

Benjamin locked his fingers behind his neck and tilted his head back. "God, Pam, this is a nightmare. I wish that were true. But I just found out that Catherine Caddaric knows about A. J., too. If she exposes our arrangement . . ." He gripped his forehead with his hand. "Listen, Liz has everything you need—all my account info, keys to my safe, my will . . ."

"Wait, wait, hold on. I don't need to hear any of that now. Who's Catherine, and why would she expose you?" Pam wasn't about to admit she'd retrieved the invitation from the trash.

"She's the founder of a group called the Brazilian Grove," said Benjamin. "It's the female version of the Bonham Grove, no men allowed. They've only been around a fraction of the time Bonham has, but they're powerful as hell and just as devious. Catherine hates everything about the Bonham Grove, so exposing me would make her year. In a way, she'd be doing them a favor by getting rid of a mole, but Catherine's hatred is multifaceted. The two of us never got along personally. Plus, revealing me has another upside—the Bonham Grove would be thrown into chaos and suspicion for quite a while. Surely they'd wonder if I was the only one."

"How do you know she knows that you were A. J.'s source?"

Benjamin placed both his hands on her shoulders and looked her directly in the eyes. He'd taken this stance when he told her about her mother, about the crash that meant she wouldn't be coming home. "She told me herself. Catherine doesn't make threats, just promises, and she always keeps them. When she tells the Grove what I did, they *will* kill me. They have no choice."

It took a moment before Pam comprehended the true meaning of his words. As they stood in the center of the hall, she hung her head and stared at the carpet. She was at a loss for words.

"Don't spend any time worrying about that, sweetie. You know your dad. I'm too goddamn mean to go anywhere." He placed one finger under Pam's chin and lifted her head. "Now back to the original question."

Pam sniffled and wiped the back of her hand across her face. "Oh yeah, why were you asking me about Alex?"

"Well, that ties back to Catherine, too. Yesterday, I spotted her with her little entourage in the lobby. They're here for the rally, too. Right there with her was one of Alex's friends. His best friend."

"Li?"

"Yes, Li."

"Are you sure, Dad? Have you even met Li?"

Benjamin pulled a photo out of his pocket. "No, but I know his face from this. It was him; I'm sure as I can be. Something is up, sweetie, and it isn't good."

Pam looked at the photo. Against the backdrop of the Brown campus, Li was all smiles next to his best friend. Alex was leaning against him, an elbow propped up on Li's shoulder.

Benjamin passed her his cell phone. "Took this to be sure."

The cell phone photo showed a silver-haired woman talking to a muscle-bound Asian woman. Just off to their right stood Li. Pamela immediately recognized his profile.

"I took it just the other day. Catherine is into some pretty wicked stuff, Pam. And if Li is in her circle, there's a good chance Alex is, too."

CHAPTER 32

The next day, Pam crossed the street from the hotel to the convention center. The brisk flow of people on the sidewalks was nothing like downtown Dallas. There, you could walk from the West End district to the JFK museum without bumping into a single person, but in downtown DC, you couldn't help brushing against at least a few passing strangers.

She hoped a short stroll would help her gather her thoughts. As she weaved in and out of the passing crowd, she found herself looking about for watchful eyes, followers, but willed herself to stop looking over her shoulder. Relatives of the Chinese president had nearly caught her just the day before, so she had to stay vigilant, but allowing her nerves to take over would only put her at a disadvantage. She had to stay calm and find a way out.

Looking up at the massive Walter T. Wallace Convention Center momentarily took her mind off the attack. The glass and granite construction took up several blocks in the city's center. She felt hypnotized as she marveled at the sleek lines of the urban architecture.

Before she knew it, she'd been drawn inside the grand lobby of the convention center. The spacious, airy interior gleamed brightly with sunlight. Flawless wood walls curved around the space, in which art hung liberally. Pam was filled with the urge to explore, to lose herself in each of the paintings.

After wandering the bottom level of the building for a while, she took the escalator to the second floor. High-ceilinged hallways branched off like mazes. She let herself get lost, wandering down the empty halls, sidestepping the occasional mop bucket left out by the cleaning crew. An eerie but pleasant feeling came over her as she walked the lonely passages.

After a few minutes, she'd gotten herself turned around. She made her way toward an exterior wall made of glass. Below, she saw the busy intersection of Ninth and L Streets. Her bearings regained, she made her way back toward the escalators.

When she got there, though, she felt sadness at the idea of ending her exploration. She stepped on the up escalator, letting herself be taken up even farther.

The third floor, like the second, was completely vacant, but it was much darker. The sun was setting now. She walked cautiously down the main corridor, opening a door or two to find large, empty rooms hidden behind. She wasn't sure what she'd say if someone asked her what she was doing.

At the end of the corridor was a sign that displayed a large arrow and the words *L Street Crossover*. In the direction of the arrow, a hallway yawned into the distance, even darker than the one she was in now.

As she examined the path to the crossover, deciding which direction to take, she thought she saw movement in the shadows. She looked closer, her anxiety escalating. The silence suddenly seemed oppressive. She now thought she heard a shuffle coming from the darkness.

"Hello? Someone there?" The catch in her voice betrayed her fear.

No answer.

She turned and began to backtrack, but in the distance, about fifty feet down the hallway she'd come from, she saw a dark silhouette emerge. The person stood in the middle of the hallway, arms at his side, ready to intercept her.

She spun around again, her heart pounding frantically. She would take her chances on the dark hallway. As she ran into the darkness, she smelled the pungent scent of tobacco.

Two rough hands stopped her progress as someone grabbed her arms. Her feet fell from under her, but her captor pulled her back up.

"Careful, Ms. Graham," a voice said.

CHAPTER 33

B enjamin placed a hand on the smooth wood of the convention center's wall, the dimming sunlight falling on him through the skylights. He supported himself as he tried to catch his breath. Alex, looking as fresh as he had when they'd begun the search half an hour before, placed a hand on his back.

So far Pam was nowhere to be found, and the number of people in the convention center was growing with every passing minute. People were gathering for one of the largest Wynn rallies yet. Anticipation crackled in the air.

Benjamin and Alex had combed the entire first level of the convention center. They'd covered a lot of ground, but there was no sign of Pam—or the men Alex had spotted trailing her into the building.

When Benjamin regained some strength, he turned to Alex. "You actually saw her enter the convention center, right?" Benjamin asked.

Alex thought for a moment. "I can't say she went in for sure, but she was definitely walking toward the entrance."

He'd spotted Pam from Benjamin's room on the ninth floor of the Renaissance Washington and thought it would be fun to call her and say he could see her. By the time he looked back down, he saw something new;

three men in dark suits appeared to be following her. They walked not far behind her, but all three seemed to have their eyes on her back.

Suddenly the call took on a new urgency. He'd dialed her number only to hear her ringtone—their favorite Russian piece—coming from within the room. There was Pamela's phone, sitting on the table.

"And these guys were all dressed alike?" Benjamin asked.

"Pretty much. Dark suits, a couple of them had sunglasses on but that's about all I could see from so high up."

"Did they seem like they were lurking? Or would you say they were actively pursuing her?"

"I think a little of both. They weren't letting her out of their sight, that was for sure. I only noticed because I had a bird's-eye view. I'm sure from the ground they looked more natural."

"Goddamn it. Where is she?"

Alex's phone rang. He glanced at the display but quickly put the phone away. "I'm gonna go find a bathroom."

Benjamin hid his suspicions as best as he could. The photo of Alex and Li was locked in his head, as was the image of Li and Catherine.

"I'll tell you what, let's just split up. We haven't even touched the second and third floors."

"Good idea," said Alex. "I'll run to the bathroom and then check the second floor. You wanna take the third?"

"That'll work. Just give me a call if you spot anything."

About ten paces from Benjamin, Alex pulled out his phone, touched the screen, and held it to his ear.

Benjamin watched as he walked right past the restrooms and disappeared from view, consumed by the crowd. He put aside his reservations about Alex. Whatever he was up to was going to have to take a backseat to finding Pamela.

He walked over to the elevators, feeling exhausted. At least from the third floor he could get a good view of certain parts of the lower levels. Maybe he'd spot her that way.

On the ride up, Benjamin thought about the men following his only child and cracked his thick knuckles.

When I catch up with them, there's gonna be very little talking.

CHAPTER 34

Pamela writhed in the man's grip, trying to get a look at his face. He had her turned around, and they now both faced the lit hallway she'd come from. The unspeaking silhouette of the other man slowly approached. Aside from a dark outline, the orange glow of a lit cigarette was all she could see of him. They stood in the dark and waited—for what, Pamela had no idea.

At the edge of the darkness, the silhouette beckoned them and threw his cigarette to the floor. The man who held her walked her forward.

"Pamela Graham!" The man's face was becoming clearer as her eyes adjusted to the light. The dim light illuminated a head of neat, crisply parted blond hair. "How about we have a little talk?" The manner was familiar—he had that nauseating *now-we-got-ya* tone mixed with a heavy portion of false friendliness. Pamela felt sick.

A third man emerged from the dark behind her and stood just behind the agent who'd invaded her home. She recognized him, too.

"I thought we were supposed to remain in contact?" the blond agent said. "We talked to you . . ." He looked over his right shoulder to the man behind him. "What was it? Over a week ago?" The second agent continued to stare straight ahead. The first agent moved closer to Pam, his face now inches from hers. She could smell the stale tobacco on his breath. "Over a week, Ms. Graham, and I haven't gotten anything from you. Not one damn thing."

Pamela jerked her arm but remained firmly in her captor's grasp. "Didn't you say I should have something before I called you? I've got nothing!"

He looked over his shoulder again, then back at Pamela. "You don't have anything, huh? Just happened to be here, at the candidate's final rally? To do what? You a big supporter?"

"Is that a crime?"

"Of course it's not. You can do anything you want, Pamela. Last time I checked, it was still a free country. But it's my job to keep it that way."

"Is that why you cornered me up here? To give me your job description?"

He laughed, but she could tell she'd irritated him. "Feisty, just like they say."

"Is that what you read in my file, agent? Or maybe you know from all the phone calls you've listened to."

He laughed again. "Too many spy novels, Ms. Graham. How about you answer a question for me? What would you think if every single person of interest just happened to pop up at the same place at the same time?"

Pam didn't answer.

"Oh, *now* we're at a loss for words. I'll tell you what we'll do; we'll just round all of you up. That includes you, Alexander, and your dad. I'm starting to think you didn't tell us anything because *you're* part of the plot." He lifted his eyes to the agent gripping her arm. "Don't underestimate her, and if she gets out of hand, don't hold back. We've got a few more to round up."

He turned and nodded to his partner and they started off toward the escalator down to the lobby. Pam was already brainstorming ways to escape the agent who held her; soon it would be them, one on one.

As the two other agents retreated down the hall, Pam saw a dark figure barrel out of the shadows toward them. The new arrival decked the agent who'd remained silent and he fell to the floor.

The blond agent—the voice of the group—turned. He began to reach into his jacket, but he was too slow. The other man bent at the waist and plowed into the agent, driving him into the wall with a massive force. His skull cracked, and he slid to the floor, his legs twisted under him.

As the man turned toward them, Pam saw her father's face. His teeth were exposed in an animallike display of rage.

Before Benjamin could take one more step, the agent's grip tightened around Pam's arm as he whipped out a Glock 42. His finger rested lightly against the trigger, the weapon extended in his steady arm and aimed directly at her father's face.

CHAPTER 35

The idling engine of the silver Aston Martin Vantage Roadster was so soothing that it could have rocked Li to sleep as he sat parked in front of the valet booth of the Marrakech. He checked the time; one hour remained until the rally was scheduled to begin. In three more hours, he would be boarding his flight back to China.

Li ran his fingertips across the smooth mahogany steering wheel. The pearl-white rental sports car reminded him of his years at Brown University, when he would rent a different car almost every weekend. He and Alex would drive into Rhode Island and raise hell all night. He smiled, remembering the countless weekends he'd spent with Alex, back when life was filled with all-night cram sessions, weekend pool parties, and long nights of drinking. In a lot of ways he missed those days, but he was also happy to have moved on to the next phase of his life.

Pressing the button on the control panel, he raised the convertible top and waved the valet off. He just wanted to sit and savor the moment for a while.

Within seconds, his solitude was interrupted by the ringing of his phone.

"Hello?"

Silence. Then a voice crackled through. "Li?"

Even through the bad connection he recognized his father's voice. "Yes ... Father?"

"Li, are you okay?"

"Yes, I am very well. My flight returns tonight. I will be back in Beijing by morning."

"Good. This is good," President Bin said before coughing heavily. "When you return, we have much to discuss."

"Yes, I understand," Li said.

His father continued, telling Li between labored breaths of his negotiations with their allies. He stressed how important it was that Li assist Catherine in any way he could, and then asked a few questions about Zhao. It was becoming clearer how much his father relied on him.

After he hung up, Li smiled. This time he really did understand what his father meant by "soft power." The byzantine deals devised by his father, the secret organization in his country formed solely for the purpose of perpetrating cyber-attacks on other countries and selling off the US dollar in order to crash the US stock markets. The byzantine deals were helping them amass oil reserves, stocks, real estate, manufacturing assets, and precious metals. It was genius and it all served one purpose. Li basked in the growing comprehension of how it all worked. He was prouder than ever to be a part of the Bin family.

His people understood the necessity of retaining power. Catherine understood it, too, and now so did he. There are no friends, no enemies, and no judgments. It was all about power. If his country didn't take it, another country would.

He let the convertible top back down. The tires on the Aston Martin spun, and the scent of burning rubber drifted into the air behind him. He darted in and out of traffic as he barreled down New York Avenue, overjoyed at his father's growing acceptance. The crisp East Coast wind felt like an old friend.

Ten minutes later he pulled into the private parking garage below the Wallace Convention Center. He parked and made a call, still seated in the car. Catherine answered after the first ring.

"Hello, Li," she said, a smile in her voice.

"Hello, Ms. Caddaric. I just parked my rental at the convention center.

I wanted to see if you could make arrangements for me to buy it and have it shipped to China."

"No problem with that, Li," she said. "Just pass the keys to my assistant and I'll take care of everything. It will be my personal gift to you."

"I can't accept something that big, Ms. Caddaric," Li protested.

"I insist, Li. It's not a problem at all."

"I am speechless. All I can say is thank you!"

"Don't think of it. You'll be up soon?"

"On my way."

Li rode the elevator up to the VIP seating section located in a balcony that overlooked Hall E of the convention center. A security guard greeted him as soon as the elevator doors opened and motioned for him to remain in place. Off to the left, Li spotted Catherine, wine glass in hand, chatting with a small group of females. She looked up and saw him at the door.

"It's okay!" Catherine shouted to the guard from across the room. "He's with us."

Li made a direct line to the private bar and ordered a drink before he took a seat. The VIP balcony gave everyone in the section an unobstructed view of the stage and of the enormous monitors on both sides of the auditorium.

Li looked on as Catherine exchanged handshakes and smiles with the VIP guests, who totaled about twenty. She would even occasionally wave to someone in the general seating area below. He couldn't help noticing that she looked like she was the one running for president.

On the stage at the front of the hall, workers scrambled back and forth, making last-minute adjustments. The giant monitors played soundless Wynn-sponsored ads, most calling for a movement to rebuild America. Some attendees held signs bearing slogans like "Break Free from China!" and "Fire China!" He knew that were he down there with the crowd, he'd get many scornful looks, based solely on his appearance. Wynn had managed to single out his country—his family—as the root cause of America's downfall.

Watching the candidate's endless rhetoric, Li felt ready to get back home, away from America. He felt his country was being unjustly disrespected by Wynn and each person who followed him. The United States was trying to bite the hand that fed it. It's exactly what he'd tried to explain to Alex that day in the hospital room in Pamplona.

Li gritted his teeth as he recalled the conversation. How could it be clearer that this buffoon had no right to say the things he said? But Alex hadn't been able to see it Li's way. His friend had even gone as far as insinuating that China was taking advantage of its position—a comment Li regarded as a direct criticism of his father.

To hell with Alex.

The playing field was about to be altered, and this entire crowd had no idea. Li vowed to remember the looks of disapproval, the signs, and the videos when it was all over.

CHAPTER 36

Benjamin Graham, staring down the barrel of a handgun, lifted his hands in surrender. Pamela remained helpless in the agent's grip. She twisted her body away from him with all her might, but she couldn't break free.

"Careful," the agent said. "You don't want to make my weapon go off, do you?"

"Don't listen to him, Pam. He's not going to shoot anyone. He's just an agent. Trust me, they shoot more pictures than bullets."

The agent's expression remained unreadable. "You sure about that?" His voice was dark and soulless, absent of any compassion or fear.

Pam was sure he was about to pull the trigger. Making a split-second decision, she rammed her elbow into the agent's ribcage as hard as she could.

To her surprise, his body felt like a rock. The agent's only reaction was to take a small step to the side, but he quickly regained his balance. He had to be wearing a bulletproof vest.

The gun remained trained on its target, the agent's arm fully extended, set to fire. Pamela felt the agent release her and step back. He was now standing a few feet back, his aim alternating between her and her father every couple of seconds.

He tossed his head to the right. "Get over there, next to him."

Pamela lifted her hands and followed his orders. She stood next to her father feeling that the luck she'd once had had finally been depleted. Her father was panting like he'd just run a marathon.

"You okay?" she whispered.

He didn't answer. Pamela looked over at him to find that his eyes were distant and glazed over. She wasn't sure he'd even heard her. He was per-spiring heavily as he swayed back and forth. *Please don't pass out, Dad.*

The agent seemed to be thinking—probably about whether to kill them or not. For the second time in two days, she grappled with the possibility that these might be her final breaths.

She narrowed her eyes, peering into the darkness behind the agent. *Am I hallucinating?* The outline of a figure seemed to lurk there. *Mind's playing tricks on you.*

The next thing she heard was a loud thump. The Glock 42 clattered to the ground. The agent's arms flopped to his sides, and his eyelids slowly closed. He toppled to the floor, lifeless.

Alex emerged from the darkness, caressing his right hand. "He's going to wake up soon. We've gotta get out of here."

Pamela still didn't quite believe it. Alex had somehow done it again. "How—" she began.

Alex rushed over and hugged her tightly. "I saw those guys follow you in. It didn't look like they were up to any good, so Ben and I came here looking for you. Looks like it's a good thing we did."

Pamela brushed a piece of hair behind his ear, speechless, before turn-ing to Ben. He'd lowered his hands, but his face was ashen and he was sweating heavily.

"You're not looking so good, Dad. You okay?" Pam said as she guided him to the wall.

He wiped the sweat off of his forehead with his palm. "Yeah, yeah, I'm fine," he said with a forced grin. "Just got drained from holding my hands in the air for so long, I think."

Alex kneeled down to check each of the men scattered across the cor-ridor. "They're all out cold."

"Not too bad for an old man, right?" Benjamin said.

"Not too bad for any man," said Alex.

Pam checked her watch and stepped over one of the bodies. "We have about forty minutes till the convention starts. I'm afraid these guys being on high alert means that something's going to happen tonight. He said *we* were the primary suspects, but we all know that's not true. We've got to find who is."

Alex and Ben looked at each other, puzzled.

"Let me tell you something I should have told you a long time ago," Pam explained. "Alex, I'm pretty sure the CIA thinks you're involved in some plot. They came to my place in Dallas. Barged in, made a bunch of insinuations, and left. They never told me exactly what they were talking about, but after this, I'm sure I'm under suspicion now, too."

"Why didn't you say anything before?" asked Alex.

Pam looked away.

"Look," Benjamin interjected, "we're all going to need some serious counseling later. Right now, all three of us are on the CIA's shit list." He pointed to the men passed out on the floor. "This little incident didn't help one bit."

"What do we do now?" Pam asked.

"First order of business: Warn Wynn's camp about what you heard in Spain. I think you're right. If they were at all serious, they could strike tonight."

Alex took in every word but remained silent. Benjamin couldn't help wondering whether Alex knew more than he was letting on, but he decided to let it go for now. Alex had seemed genuinely surprised at Pam's revelation.

"Here's my hunch, though I'm not gonna say I'd bet my life on it. I'm just trying to put myself in these guys' shoes. If I wanted to get rid of Wynn, would I do it now or wait till after the election?"

"Well, they said *if* he won the election. That's when—"

"Right," Benjamin interrupted, "but think about it. After the election, should he win, you have to go up against the security forces of the leader of the free world. It's a lot easier to just make a go for him now. Either way, we're gonna have to bypass the guesswork and just get word to Wynn. They'll know how to handle it a lot better than we can. Alex, see if you can find the convention center's head of security. Pam and I will go see if we can get word to Wynn's people."

* * *

The agent opened his eyes. He'd only passed out for a moment, but he decided it would be simpler to lie there and listen. It certainly wasn't how he'd planned this job, but it would have to work.

The main downside was being seen by these civilians. They didn't know his real identity, so he wasn't too concerned, but he still felt like it shone an unnecessary spotlight on him.

He sat up and cracked his neck. *Son of a bitch came right up behind me.* He felt the anger boil up, but he took a deep breath to calm himself. A cool head was absolutely necessary. He reached over and retrieved his gun from where he'd dropped it.

He stood gingerly, massaging the base of his neck with one hand. Pain from the recent blow crossed his shoulder blade.

His colleagues—Agents Trowbridge and Cordas—were still out, and that's the way he needed them to remain. Cordas, the Greek one, moaned quietly. *Careful. Don't wake up. Not yet.* The prone agent's eyes remained closed. *Good.*

The man then scanned the walls and corners for surveillance cameras. Nothing. *Also good.*

Finally, he crouched down to where Agent Cordas lay. He lifted his gun over his head and smashed its butt down on the head of his colleague. Moments later, he delivered a similar blow to the blond head of Agent Trowbridge.

The plan had changed, but only slightly. In fact, maybe it was easier this way. Originally, he was going to have to slip away from the other agents, but now he didn't have to worry about their questions. He'd still have to explain where he went after coming to, but that could wait for later. Part of him wished he could just walk away from the CIA after he'd finished the job for Catherine, but he knew he needed the job as cover. The Navy Seals had been a good cover, too, but he'd served his term. He wouldn't want to go back there anyway.

The agent pushed aside thoughts of the future. There was a job to complete, and he would pull it off no matter the difficulty—just like he always did.

He stole along the darkened corridors and made his way up to the perch he'd set up three days before. It was brilliant, almost too perfect. From the perch, he had a direct view of the stage of Hall E.

Tucked away high above the crowd, far above even the balconies, he assembled the high-power rifle and settled its muzzle on the small tripod. A band played bland, upbeat rock on the stage below. He put one eye to the scope, focusing twenty-four inches above the top of the podium—the exact spot where Donald Wynn's head would be within half an hour. Pamela Graham, Benjamin Graham, and the kid would also have their time in the crosshairs of his scope, but not now. *Business before bliss.*

The agent began his mental walkthrough. *The one-minute countdown begins the moment the target moves into place. Then he takes twenty seconds to line up the crosshairs and twenty seconds to control his breathing. He and the rifle are now one. In the final twenty seconds, he listens to his heartbeat until he can feel each one. At the count of sixty, the bullet cuts through the air in a direct line toward its target.*

For most jobs, he did the walkthrough nearly a hundred times. Today, due to his unexpected delay, it would be fewer than thirty.

As he did the second or third walkthrough, he practiced with Catherine in the crosshairs, focusing on the silver head in the VIP balcony. Real targets always felt better, even when he wasn't planning on actually pulling the trigger.

CHAPTER 37

A lex had darted off, saying he thought he remembered seeing the security room when they swept the building for Pam. Now Pam and her father stood on the second floor, at the top of the escalators.

It sounded like a band was playing nearby. They could hear the thump of the bass drum and bits of melody over the elated cheers of the crowd.

"Do you know which way the rally is from here?" Pam asked.

He scratched the top of his head. "Hall E, I believe, but I'm not exactly sure. I think it's this way." He pointed down the main hall of the second floor. "I know the band sounds really close, but there are speakers all over this place. I'm pretty sure it's all the way back."

"Are we just going to . . . pull someone aside and tell them what we think is going on?"

"When we get there, just let me handle it. I think I know who can nip this whole thing in the bud. If I play my cards right, I might even be able to keep Catherine's mouth shut."

"That's the part I still don't get, Dad. What's Catherine up to? I can understand why she wants to take the Grove down. But why would she even care about the election, getting into some plot with Li, and—"

"Think about it, Pam. Li's father is the president. She cares because she's on their team. I saw her portfolio, and most of her investments are over in China. She's going to make sure she's on the winning side when the dust clears. She'll use every ounce of her power to keep China happy and her investments safe. She'd even—"

"Sell out her own country," Pam finished. "We have to let someone know now, Dad. It may not be happening tonight, but we can't take any chances."

They took off down the corridor until they reached the second-level L Street walkway. "There we go," said Benjamin, pointing her toward a sign indicating that Hall E was across the way. As they speed-walked across, Pam watched the cars zipping by below.

On the other side, Pam pulled ahead of her father and took a right, following the sign that pointed them toward Hall E. Her fear had turned to excitement. Finally everything was falling into place. Her dad knew what do to—as soon as they got there, everything would be in his hands. She'd be able to breathe easy again. The crisis would be averted, and the CIA would get off her back. Chaos would return to order. Maybe she'd even reconsider joining her father at Graham Publishing. She had to admit they made a hell of a team.

Pam could see a throng of people gathered outside what she assumed was Hall E. She was now nearly running.

"Almost there!" she shouted, turning back to check on her father.

She stopped in her tracks, horrified.

He lay at least fifteen feet behind her, stretched across the floor just outside the entrance to Hall D. He was gasping for air. One hand clutched feebly at his chest.

CHAPTER 38

The plaque affixed to the light oak door read "Dale Gunner—Building Security." Alex burst into the office without knocking. The chair behind the cluttered desk was empty, but at the end of a short hallway, a line of light glowed at the bottom of a closed office door. He moved quickly to the room and swung it open. Empty.

Damn it!

He walked out of the office and scanned the area. He was in a narrow back hall with granite floors. No one in sight, but he could hear muffled live music. He figured he was now adjacent to the rear of the chamber where the rally would take place.

Alex padded down the deserted hall and slipped through a door labeled "Employees Only." He was now in a short passageway that ended in a grated staircase. At the bottom of the stairs was a gray, featureless door.

He jogged to the door, eased it open, and stepped inside. When the door closed behind him, Alex heard a prominent click. He pressed down on the inside handle to find it locked. He gave the door a hard shove, but it wouldn't budge. *Guess I'm not going back that way,* he thought.

The room he'd entered looked like it hadn't been touched in years. Cables, boxes, file cabinets, and electronic equipment were stacked everywhere, all coated with dust. The room was dusky, illuminated only by a pale block of light at its other end. Occasional thuds sounded above him, and the music was now quite loud. *I must be under the stage,* Alex thought.

He moved cautiously toward the light at the other end, picking his way through the debris. As he approached he saw that the light came from a partially open door. He could now hear voices outside.

The first man passed by the opening in a blur. More followed, all dressed in dark suits but moving more slowly than the first. Their dress made Alex hang back; they could be security, but they could also be pissed-off CIA agents.

One man stopped at the door and peered inside. Like the others, his hulking frame was clad in a dark suit. Although Alex was positive that the man could not see him in the dark, he stepped behind a tall file cabinet and watched the door as he peeked out from behind it.

The man continued to stare into the room for a moment, then reached up to touch his ear. A wire ran from his earpiece to the back of his head, disappearing somewhere below his collar. He looked a lot like a Secret Service agent. This was exactly whom Alex needed to talk to.

The man turned from the room but remained in the doorway. Alex soon saw what had drawn his attention: Strolling past the doorway was a stern-looking Donald Wynn. *He's about to go onstage!* thought Alex. *I've got to—*

He snapped out of his trance and bolted from his hiding place. As he raced for the light, the Secret Service agent reached out and pulled the door closed, oblivious to his presence. Alex was instantly consumed by pitch-black darkness.

Blind, Alex stumbled over what felt like a stack of folded cardboard boxes. He came down on his knee, aggravating the tender muscle in his thigh. He cursed under his breath, more out of frustration than pain, and continued feeling his way toward the door.

He fumbled to the spot where he thought the door had been only to find a shelf. He knocked over a pile of something, and a rain of tiny plastic objects fell to the floor. Dust now covered his fingers, and he coughed hard, trying to clear his throat of particles. He slid to the right, hands gripping the drywall in search of the door. He could still hear faint voices, but he was no longer sure exactly where they came from. All he knew was he had to get out—fast.

"Hey!" he shouted. "Hey! Can you hear me out there? *Hey!*"

The sound of the men's voices drifted farther away, eventually dwindling to nothing. Alex slammed the palm of his hand onto the wall several times. He screamed in frustration, beating the walls wildly with both hands.

CHAPTER 39

More and more people piled inside the convention center, filling the rows of seats quickly. From the moment he took his seat in the balcony, Li had kept a close eye on the crowd below, searching for anything that looked out of place. He was particularly on the lookout for anyone who looked even slightly like Alex. He mentally divided up the room and analyzed it sector by sector.

Before long, Catherine took a seat next to Li. Zhao remained by the entrance to the balcony, standing guard. Catherine loved having her around, but Li preferred traveling alone; the idea of a female sent to protect him had never sat right with him.

"Less than fifteen minutes now and we can get this show under way," Catherine said.

Li had never actually given voice to the event he was almost sure would take place tonight. Mustering all his courage, he decided to get it out in the open. He was tired of being on the sidelines. "Zhao told me you've already hired someone to take care of this," Li whispered. "Is it going to happen now?"

He'd expected her to dance around the issue, to cloak her answer in ambiguity, but she responded immediately. "Oh yes, you can set your watch to it. The guy I have on this is the quintessential pro. Nothing on this little blue planet will stop him once you've got him on the payroll."

Her words confirmed what his inner voice had been telling him all along. *Yes, this is really going to happen—tonight.* He looked away from Catherine, worried his eyes might show reservation.

She placed her veined hand on his. "Listen to me, Li," she said maternally. "The People's Republic of China will become more powerful than you can imagine. That kind of power never comes easy, but it's always worth it. You're going to lose friends, and you'll have to do a lot of things that may go against what you feel is right. However, you must remember that this is for the people of your country, the family you will have one day, future generations far past your own, and the father who has dedicated his life to the success of you and your country. This is your destiny, Li. Surely you have thought of becoming far greater than you are now."

"Yes. Most definitely."

"All that we are and become is the result of what we think." She tapped her head with her finger. "The mind is everything. What we think, we become."

"You're quoting Buddhism? I thought you were atheist."

Catherine smiled warmly. "Dear, dear. I can quote Bill Clinton without being a Democrat, right?"

"Another good point," he conceded.

A woman rushing down one of the aisles below caught Li's attention. She stopped when she reached one of the security guards, grabbing his shoulder and pointing frantically back toward the door. When she turned, he saw her face. *What are you doing, Pamela?*

Li sat up to get a better view. He was sure it was her, but Alex was nowhere in the area. *I know you're here somewhere, my friend.* Pamela's strange behavior sealed his suspicion that they were at the rally for a purpose. An unease spread over him; how could he just wait and see what happened? As much as he kept telling himself he didn't care, he did—to a point. He needed Alex to stay away.

"Catherine, excuse me for a moment? I'm going to speak to Zhao, then run to the men's room. I'll be right back."

"Sure." Catherine smiled.

When Li got out of his seat, only the broad strokes of his idea were in place. By the time he had reached Zhao, he'd developed what he felt was a flawless plan.

"Zhao, let me use your phone."

She passed it to him without question and watched, disinterested, as he dialed.

"Who you call?" she asked.

"No one. Just sending a text."

Zhao squinted, suspicious. "You text on my phone? Not yours? Who you call?"

Li ignored her as he thumbed the keys. He scanned the message for errors before transmitting it and handed the phone back to Zhao.

"If anyone texts you back, let me know, okay? I'm headed to the bathroom. Be right back."

Li hurried past the guard. Before he reached the stairway, Zhao called after him.

"Who suppose text you back?"

CHAPTER 40

Alex's phone buzzed in his pocket, and when he pulled it out it shone through the inky darkness like a beacon in the night. He castigated himself for not thinking to use the phone as a light source. On the glowing display, a text message from an unrecognized number awaited him.

"It's Pam. Texting from a disposable cell I bought after the CIA started after me again. Where are you?"

Alex's held the phone out like a faint torch. It easily illuminated the door he'd been fumbling for in the dark. It stood just feet from him.

He turned the knob and pushed. Nothing. He tried again, this time turning the knob in the opposite direction. Again, nothing. He slammed his hand against the door so hard that pain shot up his right arm.

Defeated, Alex turned his attention back to the phone. His fingers raced across the miniature buttons as he composed a reply. "Stuck under the stage. Security office was empty. You guys keep trying to get word to Wynn. I'll find a way out of here."

* * *

Zhao walked to the edge of the balcony. She spotted a door at the front of the room, at the left of the stage, and betted that, through it, she'd be able to get to the room Alex was in. She couldn't wait to get to him and nip the problem in the bud. *Remain calm, Zhao,* she kept thinking. Anger could cause her to lose focus, overreact, and possibly derail her mission. After taking care of Alex, she was going to have to have a talk with President Bin about Li. She was beginning to seriously doubt his decision-making abilities.

Zhao exited the balcony and rushed down the stairs. In the concourse outside Hall E, hundreds of people milled around. Zhao stopped when she saw a commotion. The crowd made way for three paramedics, who shouted for room as they rushed past.

Zhao was about to pull open the door to walk into Hall E when she heard a passing security person speak into his radio: "We have a Mr. Benjamin Graham, who's collapsed outside the event. His daughter's with him, but we need to page Alexander Dezcallar de Mazarredo."

Zhao changed her course and stalked behind the man, following him in the direction the paramedics had run. She joined a crowd of onlookers and squeezed far enough to the front to see what was going on. An older, thickset man lay prone on the carpet next to a gurney. Paramedics bent over him, and a slim blonde held his hand. The man seemed to be on the edge of consciousness, and Zhao saw him shake his head of thin, frazzled white hair in an effort to stay alert. A female paramedic attempted to place an oxygen mask across his face, but he pushed it away.

As she stepped even closer, the crowd parting around her, she realized she'd seen this man before. Yes, he was the enraged man from the hotel bar, the one who'd approached Catherine.

Zhao watched as he passed the woman his phone and, fighting to lift his head, spoke quietly in her ear.

Zhao quickly made an impromptu adjustment to her plan. First Pamela, then Alex.

* * *

Fighting back tears, Pamela pleaded with her father. "Come on, Dad, they're trying to help you. Let them put the mask on."

As the paramedics loaded Benjamin onto the gurney, he reached into his pocket, pulled out a cell phone, and held it out toward Pam. When she took hold of it, he pushed it into her palm, pressed her fingers around it, and took three deep breaths before he spoke. "I need you to call someone now." He paused to take in more air. "Call now. You need help."

"I will. Just relax and—"

With great effort, he propped himself up on one shaky elbow. "This is important, Pam. You have to call her now. It's under 'M. V.'" He dropped back onto the gurney, drained of strength. The paramedic placed the oxygen mask on his face. This time Ben offered no resistance.

Pamela patted her father's arm. "I'll call, Dad. And I'll be at the hospital as soon as I can."

He nodded and balled his hand into a loose thumbs-up as he was rolled toward the front entrance.

Pamela walked back toward Hall E, already scrolling through her father's contact list for the mysterious initials.

CHAPTER 41

A lex circled the cavernous room, using the light from his cell phone as a guide. He inspected each wall, shifting aside the dilapidated cardboard boxes that littered the space, but no hint of another exit presented itself.

Finally he took a seat atop a column of five stacked chairs, dejected. He felt utterly helpless. *How could I be so stupid as to get locked under here? A man's life is at stake.*

He was troubled by the thought that Pam may have wondered whether he was part of the Bin family's plot. On the last phone call he had with Li, Alex had pressed for answers about what was going on. Li refused to reveal any details, but Alex didn't need him to. Deep down, he already knew.

Guilt had weighed on his conscience since the day he overheard—or thought he overheard—the plot. He had a knack for languages, and this wasn't the first time he'd overheard a conversation not intended for his ears. He generally abided by a self-imposed rule to keep what he heard quiet, but this time he wondered whether not saying something was the right thing to do.

The investors meeting at the Eurostars Madrid Tower was not the first time he'd met the Bin brothers. Months earlier, Alex had paid a visit to Beijing, and Li had introduced him to his father, as well as his father's two brothers and various other cousins. The entire family spoke English, so it was the primary language spoken around Alex during the trip.

Over a family lunch one day, he'd struck up a conversation with the president's two brothers and found them friendly and inquisitive. When the conversation turned to business and Alex's plans to work at Mazarredo, Alex invited them to the investors meeting in Madrid. They had eagerly accepted.

On the night before Alex was to fly out of China, he attended a dinner in the grand hall of President Bin's mansion. Li had just left for a trip to Venezuela, but Alex felt comfortable enough with his friend's family to go to the event on his own.

Throughout the dinner, the presidential family talked about oil investments, the exchange rate, and even global warming—all in English. A few side conversations between President Bin and his brothers took place in Mandarin, but they were short and respectful.

Then, out of the blue, President Bin tossed his fork onto his plate. He pointed to the younger, shorter brother and began an anti-American rant in Mandarin.

"The Americans are so stupid!" he fumed. "You know what they will never understand? We don't fight wars. We win wars without confrontation. We observe, secure our place, hide our capabilities, maintain a low profile, and never ask for leadership. We secure an economic model, financial leadership, technological leadership, and then military power. We attack like a parasite would. That's why the Americans will never see us coming."

After the rant, the younger Bin brother had turned to Alex with an uncomfortable smile. "The president was saying that he dislikes American food."

Alex nodded politely.

"Pardon us if we revert to our language from time to time," he continued. "My family sometimes finds it easier to express their thoughts in our native tongue."

"No problem at all. My father and I jump into Spanish all the time."

About an hour after the president's outburst, the diners had moved to an adjacent sitting room for drinks. Surrounded by colossal bookcases and elaborate tapestries, they chatted cordially while a television, set to a news channel, played in the background.

The room fell silent when a report about Donald Wynn's candidacy came on the screen. An unflattering picture of Wynn was placed in the upper right corner of the screen as the reporter spoke of Wynn's latest criticism of China's policies. Polls indicated that he had a fighting chance of taking the highest office in the nation.

President Bin's jovial expression had vanished instantaneously when the report began, and he grunted at the television, muttering in Mandarin. Alex sloshed the wine around in his glass, pretending he had no idea what was being said. President Bin kept repeating how insulting Wynn's statements were, and then he dropped the bombshell.

He gave the simple order to the younger brother: "Call Catherine. We cannot wait any longer. Have it done before the election."

By the look in the president's eyes, there could be no question as to what "it" referred to. Pure, unadulterated hate filled the eyes of Li's father until the news report ended and Wynn's smiling face was off the screen. Alex didn't want to believe it, but whether he liked it or not, he was almost certain he'd been made privy to a deadly plot—one that would alter the course of history, probably in a dramatic way.

Now, trapped under the stage where the man himself would stand, Alex knew without a doubt that the words spoken by Li's father were not just an idle threat. It was happening right here, right now. What Alex didn't know was how big a role Li played in all of this. Was he kept out of the loop? Was he tangentially part of it? Or was he actively organizing it?

He couldn't help but wonder whether he should have spoken up when Benjamin and Pam were discussing the plot. It was the perfect opportunity to let them in on what he knew, but he hadn't said a word. Out of instinct, he'd kept the knowledge to himself.

As he sat, rethinking his decision to conceal the Bin family's intentions, he pressed the button to turn on his BlackBerry, hoping Pam had texted him back. There were no new messages.

He once again shone the light from the phone around the room. This time he noticed the faint outline of a hatch in the floor just beyond his feet. A thick black latch held it closed.

He kneeled, traced his finger along the outline of the hatch, and felt a pair of dusty hinges.

He stuck his fingers through the latch and pulled, the metal hinges shrieking as it opened. The small door was heavy, and he let it slam to the floor on the other side. A rickety-looking set of wooden stairs led down into the darkness. Alex stepped down into the dank air.

At the bottom of the steps, the darkness was even more complete. He tapped the front of his BlackBerry and brought it to life. Next to a battery icon, the screen showed "9%." *Great.*

The narrow, concrete passage he stood in ran straight ahead with no end in sight. A gray electrical box hung on the wall next to him. He opened it and flicked several switches, hoping one would light the area. The fourth switch he tried turned on a row of bare bulbs in the ceiling and cast dim light over the area.

Above his head, through the hatch, the muted racket of the band stopped abruptly. He now heard a voice over the intercom: "Technical difficulties . . . fixed right away."

Alex realized he'd likely flipped off the power on stage and caused the technical difficulties himself. *Good,* he thought. *That will delay the proceeding for a while, at least.*

He took off down the airless passage. *With any luck, I'll find another way out.*

The blackness receded before him as he walked. Just when he thought the passageway would never end, the light of his phone illuminated another set of steps that led up to a door. He stomped up the stairs and paused before trying to turn the doorknob.

Please be unlocked.

CHAPTER 42

Pamela scrolled through the list of contacts five at a time, amazed by the amount of people her father had in his phone. Finally she got to the Ms, but there was no entry for "M. V." Skipping down to the Vs, she found a Mark Vales, a Matthew Vince, and a Mitchell Von. *Seriously?* she thought, not sure how she could call any of them and explain herself—especially if she didn't get the right one the first time.

Then, on a hunch, she scrolled all the way back to the top of the list. Sure enough, there were about ten contacts listed by initials only; she'd missed it entirely the first time. There, right after the "L. K.," were the initials "M. V."

Still standing outside Hall E, Pam tapped the contact to make a call. She was exhilarated by the prospect of having an ally. The phone rang three times, then cut to a recorded message: "Please leave a message after the tone." She tried again with the same result.

Guess I'm really on my own here, she thought. *And where is Alex?*

Fighting back the onset of panic, she tried to regroup. She'd just have to pick up where her father left off. Somehow—no matter how she did it—she was going to have to get to Wynn's people and let them know that his life may be in danger. If they took her seriously right off the bat, fantastic. If they didn't, she was just going to have to find a way to make them believe her.

She walked down a hallway to the south end of Hall E and managed to find what she thought was a back entrance. The door read "Employees Only," and the round metal knob was locked.

As she moved away, she heard the sound of the crowd grow louder. She turned—a lanky bald man had walked out of the door she'd just tried. Fortunately the door closed behind him slowly, and she slipped through without being seen.

Inside she found a maze of hallways with no signs to direct her. Taking a guess, she walked down the hallway to her left.

"Excuse me," a male voice said behind her. She spun to see a young security guard with a pitted face. "You have an employee badge?"

Behind him, two men emerged from another doorway, followed by Donald Wynn himself. The three of them stopped outside the entrance to the stage, the bodyguards keeping a wary eye on Pam.

"No, I don't, but—"

The security guard pushed her back. "This way. You need to leave this area now, ma'am."

Pam pointed over the guard's shoulder. "Listen, I know, I know, but I just need to talk to him for two seconds. That's all I need—two seconds."

"Not gonna happen," he said, pushing her.

Pam could hear the amplified words of the speaker on stage: "Just a few brief words before the man of the hour himself comes out here. Please bear with us. We're experiencing some technical difficulties. We'll be delayed just a bit, but we will get this under way as soon as possible." The crowd rumbled discontentedly. "I know what you're thinking," the speaker said, doing his best to affect a light manner. "Yes, we did pay the electric bill." The audience, unamused, broke into an impromptu chant, simple but forceful: "Wynn! Wynn! Wynn!"

The security guard continued to drive Pam backward. He ushered her back out the door she'd come through and closed it tight behind her.

Discouraged but still determined, she made her way back to the front entrance to Hall E. Most of the people had gone inside now. Only a handful of people lingered outside, most of them security guards. Pam was at a complete loss as to what to do next.

She was about to walk back into Hall E when the phone in her pocket vibrated. A text message had been sent to her dad's phone. It was from contact M. V.

"Standing outside the main entrance to Hall E," read the text.

A woman dressed in light, high-waisted jeans and a stylish purple blouse stood about ten feet from Pam, cell phone in hand. The woman craned her neck down the hallway, not paying a bit of attention to Pam. Pam guessed she was close to fifty.

Pam walked up and extended her hand. "Hello, I'm Pamela Graham. Are you supposed to be meeting Benjamin Graham?"

The woman looked Pam up and down. "I'm not sure what you're talking about."

"He's my father. He asked me to call you."

The woman eyed her cautiously. "Where's your father?"

"He was taken to the hospital just a few minutes ago. He collapsed. I'm praying he just got worked up. Before they took him, he insisted I get in touch with you."

"I see." Pam could see that the woman was still reluctant.

"He said you may . . . that you might be able to help us? With what's—"

The woman broke in, apparently having decided to believe her. "I pray I can help you." She extended her hand. "My name is Marisol Vega. Let's step over here. I have a lot to tell you in a very short period of time."

CHAPTER 43

"So you're telling me there's *nothing* we can do to stop this?" Pam asked. She and Marisol had moved down the concourse outside Hall E, distancing themselves from any potential eavesdroppers.

"Sadly enough, that's correct. Once hired, this guy *will* get his target. That's what he does, and there's no one better. I don't know how he does it, but he somehow manages to get past any security team in the world."

Pam folded her arms and looked to the side, thinking. "This can't be. How do you know all this?"

"I was one of them, Pam. I was a member of the Brazilian Grove, and at one time I was proud of it. Eventually I saw the mistake I'd made, but once you become a member, it's for life. There's no resigning once you know all their secrets. The only reason I found out about their latest ploy was because there are still a few members who don't like the direction the organization is headed. I saw what they are just realizing a long time ago. They keep in touch with me—secretly, of course." Marisol looked off into the distance. "It was supposed to be a group of powerful women placed together to counter what we all disliked about the Bonham Grove, their vicious little boy's club. Now . . . well, now—"

"Ms. Vega, I'm not trying to be rude, but it sounds like you guys *are* the Bonham Grove now."

Marisol laughed gently, but Pam saw the deep sadness in her eyes. "Yes, I'm afraid so. You start an organization because you hate the way the other organization is conducting itself, but before you know it, you're just like them. We're like the pigs in *Animal Farm*, walking upright and acting like the humans they so detested."

"Ms. Vega, I'm curious—you said that there's no way to get out of the Grove once you're a member, but . . . here you are. How'd you do it?"

"Oh, you can get out all right—once you die." Marisol pulled her hair back to reveal a swath of naked, scarred scalp just above her right ear. "So that's what I did. I died. Well, for twelve and a half minutes anyway. That's what they told me when I woke up."

Pamela brought her hand to her chest and gasped. She suddenly felt she was talking to a ghost. "Oh my God, was that from a gunshot?"

"Yes, I'm afraid so, although I don't remember too much of what happened. I wasn't totally coherent again until several months afterward. I was transferred to a facility in Brazil. I did some intense rehab there. Even now I'm not quite a hundred percent, but I'm getting pretty close." She sighed softly. "I have very few outside contacts, and everyone assumed I was dead. Of course I kept it that way. Now I'm fed information by someone I trust dearly. I've managed to stay out of the spotlight for some time now."

"Is that why you're here? Your contact in the Grove alerted you to what Catherine is up to?"

"Yes, but trust me—it's not just her up to something. She has an entire country with a vested interest in Wynn's demise. She's just facilitating. She doesn't give a damn about who's in office, as long as it's to her advantage. She has a lot of money and time invested with China, and has for some time now. She bought into their thirty-year world-war plan and positioned herself to be on the winning side—with a nice profit to boot."

"Thirty-year war?" Pamela asked. It sounded like a joke, the ranting of a conspiracy theorist. "When exactly is that supposed to begin?"

"My dear, it already has." Marisol sat on a bench against the wall of the concourse and patted the space next to her. "Let me give you the broad strokes of what we're going to be dealing with."

Pam sat, unsure she wanted to hear this.

"The war started when China began selling products to the US below

cost to drive out local businesses," Marisol continued. "Just as they anticipated, this triggered a financial domino effect. Costs climbed up, so they
devalued the yuan, which stonewalled producers in Europe and the US and
pushed them out of the market."

"My dad's been saying that exact thing for years," said Pam. Indeed, the
woman sounded just like a female version of her father. "He's always saying that because of China's policies, the European and American middle
classes are tearing through their savings and mortgaging their homes just
to maintain their lifestyles."

"He's absolutely correct," Marisol said. "And guess what? Their income
hasn't increased, and it won't for a very long time. American companies
can't increase the income of the middle class and compete with the Asian
market at the same time. It's just not possible. To make things worse, 9/11
happened, and then no one was buying real estate. So the federal government drops interest rates down to nothing to prime the pump, people start
buying homes like crazy, and by '08 that bubble had burst right in their
faces. The US banks became insolvent and had to borrow about a trillion dollars from the government to stay afloat. You remember all of that,
right?"

"Are you kidding? With the great Benjamin Graham as your father, this
is the kind of stuff you have to listen to at all hours of the day."

Marisol laughed.

"But the banks did pay all that money back to the government, right?"
Pam asked.

"Yes, but that was just a dry run. Soon you had Greece, Portugal, Ire-
land, and Italy all in the same boat, trying to keep up with the rich European countries. They're hemorrhaging middle-class jobs, as we in the US
are right now. Greece was the first to default on their debt and China had
watched closely, just waiting to spring the trap they had set."

Pam shook her head. "So, to put it simply, China is waiting for the rest
of the countries to suffer the same fate as Greece. Then they'll jump in and
bail them out, since by then the banks will be owned by the government.
That means China basically . . . owns countries."

Marisol placed her hand tenderly against Pamela's face. "You're catching on, my dear."

"And since Wynn is onto them now, they can't risk him getting into office and blowing the lid off of their thirty-year plan," Pam said, beginning to comprehend the gravity of the situation.

From inside Hall E, Pam and Marisol heard thunderous applause. It sounded like the rally was finally going to start.

Both women stood.

"I know you said that there's nothing we can do to stop this, Ms. Vega, but I'm going to have to try," Pam said.

Before Pamela could take one step forward, three people emerged from a door marked "Private." In front was a woman dressed in a light-tan cashmere dress, a matching jacket, and a pearl necklace. On one side of her stood an Asian woman with a neck like a coffee can. On the other side stood a young man she'd known for years.

"Li?" said Pamela.

He didn't respond. When the silver-haired woman spoke, it was to Marisol.

"Marisol? This *is* a surprise. When my friend Zhao here told me she'd spotted you, I just had to come and see for myself. And to think, the girls and I even had a day of mourning for you!"

CHAPTER 44

Agent Trowbridge eased his body off the floor, rigid from lying in the same awkward position so long. His head throbbed and he was badly disoriented. Once he was on his feet, the hallway spun and danced before his eyes.

He gripped his head with one hand and pulled the two-way radio from the clip on his belt. "Base, this is Trowbridge."

"Go ahead, Trowbridge."

They were going to ask him questions. He looked along the floor through a painful fog. Agent Cordas was still out, his shirt collar stained with a spray of blood. "We're still at the convention center. I've got one agent down and one missing."

"Copy, Trowbridge. We've been trying to contact your team for thirty minutes now. There's another team en route. ETA two minutes."

The pounding in his head was relentless. "Copy, over."

He kneeled down next to his colleague and placed two fingers on his neck, just below the jaw. The pulse was strong, but a growing scarlet trail of blood led from his ear to the floor.

Slowly, his memory began to come back to him. Cornering Pamela, leaving her with Agent Hansen—and then, blackness.

He smacked the wall with the palm of his hand, his blood boiling. *I knew it. I knew she was part of this all along.* She was every bit the person he had read about in the file.

Pamela Graham's adventure in Russia had placed her on the CIA's person-of-interest list, and while others in the organization smiled when speaking of her escapades, as if she got a pass for kidnapping a kid from a foreign country, he took the matter more seriously. Her actions in Russia could have caused an international incident. She was a loose cannon.

I bet she and the kid are already skipping the country.

He spoke into the radio again. "Base, this is Trowbridge."

"Go ahead, Trowbridge."

"Pamela Graham is at large."

"Copy," the voice replied. "The second team is at the center now."

"Copy," said agent Trowbridge.

He searched for any type of clue that pointed toward what exactly had happened. Where the hell was Agent Hansen?

He paced the hallway, opening a couple of doors and peering inside.

He switched off the safety on his pistol and moved deeper into the dark part of the hallway, his back sliding against the smooth surface of the wall, a miniature pencil flashlight lighting his way.

When he came upon a back stairwell, the door was ajar. On a hunch, he took it up to the next floor.

At the top of the stairs a door led to a series of rooms. There was no natural light here, so he relied entirely on his penlight as he paced down the hallway. He opened a couple of doors; one contained a jumble of mops and trash bins and smelled pungently of bleach, the other looked like some kind of archive, with cassettes stacked on cheap gray shelving.

The hallway ended in a T, and to the left, Agent Trowbridge saw a glowing rectangle suspended in the air.

Trowbridge held his weapon low in front of him with both hands as he stepped down the hall. The light came from a rectangular window set at the top of a wooden door. He cautiously peered into the room.

Inside, the foreground was shadowy, but beyond a half wall glowed an immense chamber. The room was some kind of enclosed balcony. Over the edge, he could see the top half of a giant monitor; it was splashed with a waving flag in red, white, and blue. Through the door, he could now hear the hum of the crowd below.

Trowbridge raised his head and leaned closer to the window to take in more of the room's contents. As his eyes adjusted to the brightness, he made out a human form crouched behind the wall in a familiar stance. Spotlights and boxes cluttered the rest of the space.

When Trowbridge touched the door, it moved forward soundlessly. He nudged it again and it moved a bit farther. He could now hear the voices below much better.

"How about we bring him onstage?" said the announcer. "Ladies and gentleman, Donald Wynn!"

The jumbo monitor switched to a live view of the stage. The camera zoomed in on the candidate as he stepped from the side door, waving.

Trowbridge pushed the door open wider, bracing himself to be given away by a squeak at any moment. He could now see the person much better. The back of the head looked familiar. He knelt before a tripod, grasping a rifle aimed at the stage below.

Hansen?

The complete shock of the sight brought with it a full understanding of something he'd somehow already known. Hansen's obsession with privacy, his propensity to disappear at odd times, and his near-complete lack of family or friends suddenly made sense.

The monitor below now displayed an image of Wynn shaking the hand of the man who'd introduced him.

A conversation with Hansen would be useless at this point. It was clear what he was doing, and this could only end one way.

Trowbridge leveled his weapon to the back of Hansen's head without a sound.

God, forgive me.

CHAPTER 45

Though Alex was thankful to be out of the subterranean passage, he was now completely disoriented. The door at the end of the passage had been unlocked—his first bit of luck in a while. After running through several hallways, cutting across a large empty hall, and taking an inclined corridor to a garage area, he'd ended up on an elevated walkway that ran above the concourse outside Halls D and E. Had someone offered Alex a small fortune to retrace the path he took after leaving the room below the stage, he couldn't have done it.

His plan now was to walk straight into the rally, buttonhole the first security person he saw, and not let up until they had Wynn safely off that stage. Time was running out.

As he continued down the walkway, assuming he'd find stairs he could take down to the area outside Hall E, he heard animated voices from below him. Keeping quiet, he peered over the railing.

The concourse below was now deserted; everyone had made their way into the rally. In a hallway that intersected with the concourse, a small group of people stood. His heart leapt to his chest when he saw Pamela. A woman in jeans stood next to her, and facing them stood a silver-haired woman in pearls, who looked to Alex like someone's wealthy aunt. Next to her was Li.

A severe Asian woman stood behind Pamela and the casually dressed woman; it was clear she was making sure they couldn't escape.

Oh my God, thought Alex. *It's really happening.*

He remained quiet and edged slowly toward a pillar that would shield him from view of the group. Speakers positioned throughout the concourse played the racket happening in Hall E at a low volume, but Alex was close enough to hear their words. The silver-haired woman was addressing Pam. "Ms. Graham," she said haughtily, "I must say that I'm a bit disappointed. I had even sent you an invitation to be a part of my group. Many women would kill to be a member."

"Thanks, Catherine," Pam said defiantly. "I think I'll pass. I hear some women are also dying to get out."

"I can't imagine who's been spreading such vile gossip!" said Catherine, feigning surprise. "Don't tell me you've been listening to the stories of your new friend Ms. Vega?"

Alex had no idea what the women were talking about, or why Li didn't seem to be taking Pam's side. His friend stood and listened to the silver-haired woman, impassive as a rock. *After everything Pam did for him—for us*, Alex thought, picturing the gifts, the long talks, the rescues from all the trouble they got into at school.

Alex watched in horror as Pam suddenly bolted from the group.

"Get her!" the silver-haired woman said, her bitter screech contrasting sharply with her genteel appearance. The Asian woman stepped forward and placed the muzzle of her gun into the back of the woman in jeans.

Li tore after Pam, who now sprinted down the concourse, parallel to the walkway above. Alex abandoned his pillar and ran the same direction, one level above. He could see Li gaining on Pam.

The hard voice of the silver-haired woman screamed again. "Up there! That's her son, Alex, running up there!"

A bullet clanged off the railing.

"No shooting, Zhao!" he heard the woman hiss below. "What's *wrong* with you!"

Several feet ahead, a curved set of white steps led to the level below. Alex bounded down the stairs, clearing the last six in one leap. He hit the ground seconds after Li tore past, just feet from reaching Pam.

Still running at full speed, Alex saw Li reach out and grab Pam's shoulder. The instant Li touched her, Alex felt a jolt of unfiltered rage. His vision blurred, and he could feel his entire body tighten with the uncontrollable desire to wrap his hands around Li's neck and snap it.

Pam lost her balance as Li pulled her backward. Her legs shot from beneath her and she slammed against the floor.

Li stumbled toward Pam, but looked up when he heard someone running toward him. His eyes met Alex's for the first time. Before the sight could sink in, Alex sunk a forceful blow straight into Li's jaw. His friend's head snapped violently to the side. As Li fell to the ground, Alex continued his attack. He pounced on him and began pummeling his face with his fists.

Li let out a bloodcurdling scream, and convulsed his whole body. He'd managed to lift a foot to Alex's stomach and shove his attacker off.

With an angry growl, Li jumped to his feet. Blood poured from his mouth and ran down his chin. Alex was still pushing himself up from the floor when Li delivered a hard kick into his ribs.

Alex grunted and fell to his side, squirming on the floor and gasping for air. Li backed up to run at him with another kick, but Pam reached out and grabbed his leg. She stopped the kick, but he jerked his leg away and turned back to Alex.

The speakers blared with cheers from inside the hall. The sound reminded Alex why they were there, and he felt a fresh wave of strength come over him. He got to his feet. He wanted to tell Pam to go and warn Wynn's people but his lungs still ached for air. No words came out.

"You're *dead!*" Li screamed.

He charged Alex at full speed, eyes wide with madness. Alex braced himself, but Li froze when a commanding voice shouted from above. "Hold it!"

Li, Alex, and Pam all turned to see who'd spoken. Along the elevated walkway, five men in dark suits stood looking down, weapons drawn. "Stop right there!" the voice said.

Alex didn't recognize any of the men—these were different agents than the ones he and Benjamin had knocked out earlier. He lifted his hands in surrender as they descended the stairs. Li simply stared, hands at his side.

"Stay right where you are and no one will get hurt," the lead agent said. He then spoke into his radio. "Base, we have them. Check back with you in five."

As he placed the radio back in his belt, shots rang out in the concourse. Alex saw two of the agents go down instantly. The others scrambled for cover.

The Asian woman moved in fast and threw herself in front of Alex, gun roaming for the other agents.

She elbowed Li and jerked her head in the direction of the escalators that descended to the front lobby.

"Go!" she shouted.

CHAPTER 46

"Trowbridge, this is base. We just got confirmation. They got 'em. Over."

When the words came through the two-way radio still clipped to Agent Trowbridge's belt, his blood ran cold. All the training, year after year, month after month, hour after hour, was wasted when an agent made one crucial error. In his occupation, there were very few second chances.

The procedures he'd rehearsed countless times now exploded into his head. *When approaching a suspect alone, use extreme caution. Survey the area, check your rear, reassess the situation, and turn off all incoming communication.*

Trowbridge hesitated for a fraction of a second, stunned by the noise from his belt. He was no match for the fastest and most accurate agent in sixty years of CIA history. Hansen released the rifle, spun around, and pulled a handgun from his jacket. Hansen was also an excellent contingency planner; the gun was fitted with a silencer.

Before Trowbridge could think another thought, the bullet was lodged in his brain.

* * *

Hansen stood over Trowbridge. The one-inch hole in the center of his fore-head told him he didn't need to check for a pulse.

This kill was a little different than most—he'd actually known Trow-bridge. For a fleeting moment, Hansen wondered how Trowbridge's widow would handle the loss. Then there were Trowbridge's three kids; Hansen had met them just the week before at a barbecue in the Trowbridges' back-yard. He pondered their reactions with more curiosity than sadness.

Everyone in the department had assumed that he and Trowbridge were pals, buddies till the end. They would have been shocked to see that façade crumble, as it had in the tiny room overlooking Hall E of the Walter T. Wallace Convention Center. Trowbridge, like everyone else in Hansen's life, had served purely as an alibi, a cover.

As he stood over the corpse of his former friend, Hansen did feel some regret, but only for the complications this would cause. It would be difficult to stay out of the spotlight during the internal investigation that would inevitably take place. When the department began digging into the death of Trowbridge, it would get tied back to him. Being forced to leave the CIA would be a major setback in his career.

No matter how much it dismayed him, all of that would have to be addressed at another time. He still had a job to complete. He kicked the legs of Trowbridge's lifeless body. *You bastard, I had a perfect shot. Now I have to start over.*

This was the first time a job had been interrupted so dramatically. It would take some time to regain his equilibrium. The speech would last thirty minutes, so at least he had time. His heart swelled just thinking about getting back to that precious moment when everything was perfect. The alignment, focus, and breathing were all essential to becoming one with the rifle. Once there, once he reached that peak, then it was time—swish. The sweetest sound ever made.

He returned to his post and kneeled into his shooter's stance. The butt of the rifle slid into the pocket of his upper shoulder like a foot into an old pair of slippers. His index finger lightly caressed the area around the rifle's sensitive trigger.

He adjusted the crosshairs until the lines intersected at the exact spot he wanted to hit. The hardest part was containing his excitement. He needed to calm down.

The cheering finally subsided enough for Wynn to begin his speech. Occasionally the candidate's head would dip out of sight as he bent to address someone in the audience, but he always returned to his original position, right in the center of Hansen's scope.

The agent, however, had yet to calm himself and get in sync with the gun. He was still tingling from the perfect rolling shot he'd delivered into Trowbridge's forehead, and his heart was beating far too fast.

He forced himself to do a set of breathing exercises. This was one shot he couldn't miss.

CHAPTER 47

At Zhao's command, Li took off running.

Alex burst from a standstill and took after him. Shots sounded around them—the standing agents were now taking shots at Zhao, and she didn't hesitate to fire back. Alex and Li ran with no regard for the bullets flying through the concourse.

"Alex!" Pam shouted over the gunshots, but he was already too far away. He vanished at the end of the concourse as he followed Li around a corner. Catherine and Marisol were nowhere to be seen. Pam, still on the ground, scooted to the wall, ducking her head. She scuttled into an alcove just down the hall from Zhao and tucked herself out of sight behind a free-standing map of the convention center.

The rally continued over the speakers; no one in the hall seemed to have noticed the shots fired outside. Wynn's speech echoed through the building, peppered with cheers and laughter.

In the concourse, Zhao continued with her one-woman war, dodging bullets from the agents and returning fire liberally. She ducked behind a pillar to reload her weapon with swift expertise, showing no interest in abandoning the gun battle. She was in her element.

Pam wasn't about to stick around until Zhao finished with the agents and came for her. She knew she had to get away at her first opportunity.

Timing was going to be crucial, but Pamela was ready. Zhao ducked below the walkway to reload for the third time. Pamela knew that it was her time to make a break for it. She ran in the opposite direction, circling the outskirts of Hall E.

She glanced behind her, hoping she'd made it away without attracting Zhao's attention. A wave of faintness washed over her at the sight she saw behind her. Zhao had walked straight up to the corner where the two remaining agents hid. One man now lay lifeless on the hallway carpet, and Zhao was emptying her gun into the chest of the other.

Pam turned back, her legs flailing in the fastest run she could muster. After a few more seconds of frenzied running, she looked back toward Zhao's massacre. To her relief—and horror—she saw the woman running with machinelike speed away from her, in the direction Li and Alex had run.

Pam knew that Zhao's main assignment was keeping Li safe—even if that meant disposing of his best friend.

CHAPTER 48

A lex's feet pounded the ramp as he pursued his former best friend with every ounce of energy left in him. His initial adrenaline rush was fading, but he was determined to keep up the chase. Giving up would be tantamount to agreeing with what Li and his family were trying to do—to Donald Wynn, and to America. All the labels affixed to Li—*roommate, classmate, friend*—had been erased by blind rage.

As he flew down the steep ramp, Alex replayed the scene of Li dragging Pam to the ground. The image stoked his resolve; he would catch Li no matter what. What did it matter that Li had been a track star? No one touched Pam like that.

Alex had witnessed a gradual change in Li, but nothing he ever thought would lead them here. The changes had been so subtle that they were easy to ignore, but he now saw that the boy he knew in college had evolved into a different person. Perhaps it was normal for the camaraderie of two wild college roommates to run its course, but Alex had never imagined it would come to this, not by any stretch of the imagination.

For years, he'd overlooked the aspects of Li that bothered him—the extreme competitiveness, the selfish outlook, the disdain for those below him. Alex also sensed envy on Li's part—always expressed through subtle looks or uncomfortable silences, but there nonetheless.

A plan like the one Li was involved in was insane. It was premeditated murder of the most dramatic kind. Alex couldn't help wondering how much of it stemmed from Li's upbringing. Li had been conditioned to embrace the philosophies of the generations that came before him. Perhaps his father had planted something in him that lay dormant for a while but was now spreading like a cancer.

Stopping Li right now would be the first step in putting an end to the nefarious plan designed by Li's father and uncles. Alex marveled at the fact that the outcome of this night could literally change history. He wasn't even old enough to buy himself a beer.

A chance encounter with Pam had saved him from what likely would've been a life of hardship, while Li's life had been mapped out for him from the beginning. He recalled how Li, watching his friend marvel at the lavish lifestyle of the Bin family, would often say, "Silver spoons ain't free, Russian boy." They came from different worlds, and the laws of balance would eventually return them to their roots.

Whether they admitted it or not, they'd always been headed down opposite paths. Their lives had only crossed momentarily, thanks to an arbitrary room assignment by a residential coordinator at Brown University.

Part of him yearned to simply let Li go. *Why does it matter?* a part of him wondered. But another part of him told him that the chase did matter—on a greater level than he could comprehend.

Li was a part of a plan to destroy a country that had been a refuge to Alex. If he'd sunk to these depths—participating in a plot like this—at the age of twenty, who knew what lay in his future.

Shit, thought Alex as Li veered toward the parking garage of the convention center. He could easily lose his quarry in there. To Alex's surprise, Li careened around the corner of the parking garage without entering. When he turned the same corner, he saw Li running straight down the sidewalk that ran past the convention center's south entrance. Li's head swiveled from left to right as he searched for a way to lose Alex. The street, now lit by tall lamps and the light from the convention center, was empty.

Suddenly Li stopped running. Alex instinctively slowed his pace as he closed the distance between them.

Li turned. In his hand he held a small handgun, which he leveled directly at Alex.

Alex dove from the sidewalk and rolled behind a four-foot concrete wall. A bullet cracked against the top of the wall just over his head, sending up a puff of dust.

He remained crouched there until he heard Li running away. Alex stood to see Li's form receding into the darkness as he dashed across Ninth Street. He watched Li run past a pair of orange cones, shoes crunching in the loose gravel of a construction site on the far side of the street.

Li's entire body vanished in the snap of a finger as he fell straight down. A nauseating crack sounded in the still night air, followed by a meaty thump. Then, silence.

Alex jogged over to the place where Li had disappeared and slowed as he approached an open cavity in the ground. The cover of the manhole was missing entirely, and blood was splattered on the pavement around the rim. From inside the pitch-black pit, there was no movement or sound.

He stood at the corner of L and Seventh Streets, too numb to move. Four years of laughter, mischief, debates, and travels had drawn to an end. He closed his eyes and lowered his head.

The prayer was in part to properly show respect for Li, but there was another reason Alex felt the need to appeal to a greater power. A dark sequence had been set in motion, and Alex would need help if he was going to help stop it.

Behind Alex, light fell from the convention center and onto the street. A couple walked up Seventh, hand in hand, completely unaware of the freshly dead body that lay below.

I have to get inside and find Pam.

CHAPTER 49

A s Pamela approached the set of three double doors that led into Hall E, she saw two security guards dressed in ill-fitting beige uniforms, completely oblivious to the downed agents in the adjoining hall. Pale and overweight, they hardly looked like heroes, but they would do. She'd alert them, and they would get Wynn off the stage. Over the speakers in the otherwise deserted hallway, she could hear the candidate bellowing into the microphone, speaking words that she knew millions were listening to.

A conviction swept over her. Something would happen tonight to change the course of history. She could feel it, taste it. Ms. Vega's haunting words echoed in her mind: *Nothing was going to stop him. He had a job . . .*

"Excuse me, I need to speak to you for a moment," she said to the closer of the two security guards.

"How can I help you, ma'am?" he asked.

"You've got to get Wynn off the stage—*now*. The Chinese have a guy here . . . he's here now . . . he's gonna kill him!"

The security guard pushed his palms toward Pam and gave his colleague a questioning look.

"Ma'am, who are you? We've got this place on lockdown, and as much as the Chinese would love to see Mr. Wynn gone, I don't think—"

"No!" Pam screamed. "You don't get it! Shit!" She flung her arm back toward the concourse where Zhao had dispatched the men. "They just killed like five CIA agents back there! If you won't do something, maybe I can find someone more professional than a couple of washed-up, part-time security guards. We have to get him out of there *now!*"

The two security guards were now on either side of Pam, blocking her from moving toward the hall. "Now let's just calm down a moment, miss. Trust me, we've got everything under control. I guarantee you, no Chinese agent brought so much as a toothpick into this place tonight."

"Guys, listen!" Pamela pleaded. "If I'm wrong about this, we can figure it out later." She stopped, jerked her arm from the man's grasp, and walked away without another word—it was no use trying to convince these guys. *What a waste of time,* she thought.

As she walked down the concourse and rounded the curve of the hallway, she found herself face to face with one of the last people she would've expected to see.

"D-Dad?" she stammered.

"Hey, honey!" Benjamin opened his arms wide and embraced his daughter. Besides his disheveled hair, he looked completely recovered.

"Are . . . are you okay? You just collapsed!"

"I'm fine, baby. Just got a little excited. They were convinced I'd had a heart attack, but even when they saw that I hadn't, they wanted to drive me to the hospital. I managed to fight 'em off. Did you—where are we? Is—"

"We have to get in there, Dad. The guys at the front wouldn't believe me. They're just contract security. We have to get to someone who's CIA. There were a bunch of them, but this woman . . . they're all dead, the agents . . . and Alex ran off after Li."

Ben's face looked ashen. Pamela took his elbow and led him back toward where the standoff had occurred a mere five minutes before. There was a side entrance to Hall E there. Why it hadn't been guarded Pam didn't know. She just had to get in there and get Wynn off the stage.

Ben was silent as they passed the suited bodies of the agents lying on the blood-smeared carpet. The smell of gunpowder still hung in the air.

When they pushed through the side door of Hall E, they found themselves on the perimeter of the massive chamber. Every seat was filled, and people stood all along the walls. No one noticed their entrance. Wynn had the room transfixed.

Pam spotted two men standing against the wall farther back in the hall. The unmistakable agent stance that had terrified her earlier in the night now gave her hope. She motioned for her father to follow her and began pushing her way through the crowd toward them.

* * *

Agent Hansen removed his finger from the rifle's trigger. His brow wrinkled as he rotated the rifle on the tripod. The rifle's scope veered away from Wynn's head momentarily. The encounter with Trowbridge had thrown him off, and he had to get back on track, quick.

He peered straight down at the crowd, mostly on its feet now. He'd been keeping an eye on his fellow agents, dreading the mess of explaining Trowbridge's death. He caught sight of two figures making a beeline for the agents and swung his scope down to get a better view.

What in the hell are they doing there? It was the Grahams—the father and daughter he had at gunpoint just before he blacked out.

He re-aimed the rifle at the candidate's head. With one eye lined up with the scope and the flat end of the gun wedged tight against his shoulder, he began the sequence again. He had to act fast.

Alignment, focus, breathing . . . alignment, focus, breathing . . .

CHAPTER 50

Wynn's voice boomed from the overhead speakers. "You know I can't leave here without giving you my opinion of our friends over in China, right?" The cheers lasted for a full minute.

Pam elbowed her way past a middle-aged woman, not bothering to apologize. As she approached, the agents had already spotted her. She was sure they knew exactly who she was.

"Hey, guys," she said at full volume. "Get him offstage *now*. It's happening. You've got men down just outside."

A few people in the crowd turned toward her, looking annoyed. The two agents looked at each other, and one quickly brought his radio to his mouth. "Stockton. Come in," he said quietly. He stood looking at the radio expectantly. Silence.

"I don't know about you, but I don't like the fact that China's making the greatest country in the world out to be a bunch of idiots!" Wynn said. "Clearly they don't want to see someone like me in office. They know their party is over the second that happens."

The crowd had given him so many standing ovations that most people now just remained standing.

Pam looked up. High above the crowd, a bank of dark windows was set in the cream-colored back wall of the chamber. Pam scanned the area and caught a hint of movement. A tiny glint. It could've been nothing, but she knew it wasn't.

The agents were now consulting each other in low whispers.

"This is . . . It's happening! There's no time!" Pam shouted.

* * *

Agent Hansen's universe was now in perfect alignment. The focus was perfect, and he could feel his controlled breathing blend with the beat of his heart. He had arrived at the sacred moment. All he had to do was press the trigger between any two heartbeats. Then—swish. *My will be done.*

His index finger slid from the side of the housing. It glided into the hole and perched over the trigger like an eagle over unsuspecting prey.

* * *

More faces—annoyed, scandalized—turned toward the sound of Pam's outburst. She turned from the agents and began jogging down an aisle toward the stage.

"Mr. Wynn! Get down! Now! Get down!" she shouted at the top of her lungs.

The crowd gasped and mumbled, and the agents tore after Pam. Noticing the commotion below, Wynn stopped speaking.

"*Get down!*" Pam screamed again, now less than fifty feet from the stage.

Wynn didn't heed Pam's command, but he did step to the side of the podium for a better view, and five members of his personal security team sprung from the wings. As the agents rushed down the aisle and past Pam, a chunk of wood exploded from the podium. Wynn now dropped to the stage and was soon under a dog pile of security personnel. Another sharp whiz cut through the air, and a planter at the back of the stage exploded. The mass of security guards, now joined by the two agents who'd sprinted up the stairs to the stage, moved in a huddle toward the exit, shielding Wynn.

Screams sounded from the crowd, and Pam ducked to the floor. Chaos now filled Hall E. Half the crowd was making a mad dash for the exits, while the other half crouched behind their seats in fear.

Pam rose and made her way back toward her father, her steps quick, her body bent. Benjamin stood like a statue above the churning mass of people, one strand of stiff white hair standing on end at the side of his head.

"Daddy," Pam said, falling into his arms and feeling truly safe for the first time in weeks. Benjamin held her tight but didn't say a word.

Over his shoulder, Pam saw a familiar form forcing his way into the hall against the stream of terrified attendees.

Tears—of relief, of exhaustion, of fear—fell down her cheeks.

Alex. You're okay.

CHAPTER 51

Pam was still enclosed in her father's thick arms when they were roughly pulled apart by a ruddy-faced man in a dark suit. Two similarly dressed men stood at his back.

"We're going to need both of you to come with us," said the man.

Good lord—how many of these guys do they have here? Pam thought, allowing the man to jerk her away from her father. Another of the men grabbed Benjamin's arm in a rough grip.

Pam turned to the back of the hall and saw Alex, still pushing his way through the frantic crowd. She caught his eye and gave him a look, trying her best to convey her message: *Get out of here.* She knew the agents would only pick him up, too.

She saw Alex stop in his tracks. He nodded and after a split second pointed up, toward the dark set of windows set against the back wall. *I'm going*, he mouthed. *I'm going up there.*

Pam felt cold metal against her wrists, and she found herself nodding in reply even though no part of her wanted her precious Alex to embark on a foolish crusade to take down a trained assassin.

The handcuffs clicked with finality as Alex turned and ran, with the crowd this time, his sport coat flapping behind him.

The ruddy-faced man spoke into his radio as Benjamin's wrists were secured. "Got 'em. Over."

"You've got the wrong people," said Benjamin. "You're arresting exactly who you shouldn't be arresting."

"We'll see about that," said the man cuffing him.

Pamela shook her head at her father. She understood the futility of arguing any further. They'd figure it out soon and let them go. Wynn was safe—that's what mattered.

Ben and Pam were silent as the agents escorted them out of Hall E, down the concourse, out the front entrance, and toward two waiting black Crown Victorias.

Across the street, Pam spotted Catherine walking under the halo of a streetlamp. The pearls on the back of her neck glowed under her radiant silver bob. Crossing Seventh Street at M, she casually approached a black Rolls-Royce Phantom and slid into the backseat.

The car pulled away from the curb at a leisurely pace, passed right by the front of the convention center, made a right at Mount Vernon Square, and was gone.

CHAPTER 52

Darkness was now working in Alex's favor. He crept along the back
hallways of the third level, trying to calculate the best route to the
room he'd seen the muzzle flash come from. His dying phone illuminated
his steps.

He turned down a dark hallway and immediately stepped back—he'd
seen the silhouette of a tall man. He craned his neck and peered back
around the corner. The man was now running away from Alex's position.

That has to be him.

Alex tore after him. He had no specific plan, but he would catch up
with this person, whether he was a hired professional or some lackey of the
Bin family. He'd make things right, no matter what. His silence had allowed
this to go way too far.

As he ran after the man, the hallways lightened. Alex turned a corner
and saw a door closing about twenty feet in the distance. An icon affixed to
the wall marked it as leading to a stairwell, but Alex already knew that—
he'd taken this route in reverse just before he discovered Pam and Benjamin being held at gunpoint earlier that night.

Without hesitation, Alex followed the sniper down. He could hear the
man's feet scuffing against the stairs below. He looked down the center of

the stairwell and saw the sniper's hand gliding along the rail as he made his rapid descent.

At the second floor, the man kept going down. Just as Alex left the second-floor landing, he heard the slam of another door.

"Damn it!" Alex shouted when he got to the first level of the stairwell. There were two doors, neither marked, and neither bearing any clue as to whether the sniper had just passed through.

He quickly did a mental coin toss and placed his hand on the door to his right. He stopped himself and pressed his ear to the metal of the door.

Click.

He jumped back and stared at the door handle, his mind spinning. After a moment he opened the other door wide, then slammed it closed with all his might. Still in the stairwell, he slipped back to the door on the right and pressed himself up against the wall.

A second later the right-side door burst open. Alex, hidden behind the door, saw the sniper enter, his pistol extended in front of him. The element of surprise was on Alex's side. He sprung onto the man's back. One hand went over the sniper's face while the other worked to wrest the gun from his grip. The sniper roared as Alex's fingers shoved into his eye sockets.

They both toppled to the floor. The sniper fell to a crawling position, and his weapon flew across the floor. Alex fell off him and backed away, putting himself between the sniper and the gun.

With a snarl, the sniper came at Alex. Alex managed to land a blow to his face, but it did little to stop him. A powerful hand wrapped around Alex's throat as the sniper shoved him back. The edge of the stairs' metal railing dug into his back.

"That was a really goddamn *stupid* thing to do," the sniper hissed. Flecks of spittle flew onto Alex's face.

The man then kneed Alex in the gut and kicked his right leg, connecting right at the spot where the bull's horn had pierced him.

The pain was instant and excruciating. The stitches tore apart and a wet flow of blood soaked Alex's pants. His thigh tightened and twisted, an unbearable jolt racing up his entire right side.

CHAPTER 53

The mixed scent of fried food and cheap cologne wafted into the back-seat of the black federal car. The drab gray interior and missing interior door handles gave the car's backseat the feeling of a mobile prison cell. Pamela tried to scratch the back of her neck, but the handcuffs wouldn't allow it.

Base, this is team two," said one of the agents into his radio. The other was maneuvering the car away from the convention center. "We have both in custody and are en route."

"Copy, team two. We're running a background check on Pamela Graham and the kid now. I was told we had a file on Ms. Graham, but we haven't been able to locate it. We will send you more info if needed. Over."

The agents turned to each other. The one in the passenger's seat raised his eyebrows and silently mouthed, *Kid?* The driver simply stared ahead.

Yeah, guys, you got the wrong people, Pam thought.

"Uh . . . base? This is team two again. Did you say 'kid'?"

"Trowbridge called in the names and told us to place them on the watch list. Pamela Graham, age thirty-one, and Alexander Dezcallar de Mazarredo, age twenty."

The driver smacked the steering wheel with the palm of his hand. The passenger spoke back into the radio. "Base, we are headed back to the center. We still need to locate Alexander Mazarredo. Over."

"Copy," the voice said.

"Damn it!" said the passenger. "If this kid was there, he sure as hell is gone by now."

Tires screeched as the driver hit the brakes and did a U-turn. Pamela flew back against the seat. She looked back and saw the car carrying her father do a tight half-doughnut, right on their tail.

"We'll have a lot of ground to cover when we get there," said the driver.

"Damn right we will. Try two million square feet of it. Shit, this is gonna be a long night."

"It's gonna take all four of us, so . . . what do we do with them?"

"Nothing. They stay in the cars. If we have to, we can call in backup to get them."

A minute later, the pair of Crown Victorias lurched to a stop at the curb. Light from inside the convention center glowed brightly in the night; though beautiful, the glass and granite structure looked to Pam like a giant cage, with Alex trapped inside.

The four agents hustled out of the cars and ran toward the main entrance. As soon as they were out of view, Pamela twisted to look at the car parked behind her. In the dark car, she could barely make out the outline of her father's broad shoulders.

Pamela felt crushed under the weight of her own helplessness. She yanked on the handcuffs, but it only aggravated her already-chafed wrists.

In the darkness on the opposite side of Ninth Street, Pamela noticed a lone figure. The person wore a full-length coat over a dark hoodie. A scarf was pulled across the person's mouth. Whoever it was stood staring across the street, staring straight toward the unmarked cars.

What the hell? thought Pamela.

The figure stepped down into the street and began walking straight for the car that held Pam captive. Terrified, Pam leaned back and delivered several swift kicks to the door with her heel but only succeeded in making a few light scuffs on the black plastic.

Dread filled her as the person walked steadily closer, looking like a specter. From the way the person moved, Pamela gathered it was a woman.

"Oh my God, oh my God, oh my God," Pamela said aloud in the hushed backseat. She could almost see the gun that was about to be pulled on her, feel the bullet ripping through her body.

Feet from the car, the figure looked right and left and put a hand on the door handle. Pam pushed herself to the other side, preparing to deliver the hardest horse kick she could muster.

Please don't open . . . please don't open . . .

There was a click, and the sounds of the street outside rushed into the car's interior.

Before Pam could react, the figure spoke: "Pamela—it's me."

A lowered scarf revealed the face of Marisol Vega.

Pam's terror was instantly transformed to exhilaration.

"Let's get your dad and get out of here before they get back," said Marisol.

CHAPTER 54

Alex pulled away and lifted his hands as he lay on the floor, blood seeping from his leg.

"I'm . . . I'm unarmed."

"Doesn't matter whether you're armed," the shooter replied. He lifted the gun toward Alex's face.

Alex swept his leg across the floor and connected with the shooter's ankle. The bullet hit the floor just over the top of his head and ricocheted through the far wall. The last martial arts class Alex had taken was more than three years ago, while he was still in prep school, but his extensive training kicked in as if he'd been in class yesterday.

The shooter jumped to the side, swinging the gun toward Alex. The next move had already been prepared. Using only his arms, Alex lifted his body into the air legs-first and delivered a side kick into the chest of the shooter. The gun flew out of his hands and slid across the floor as the sniper fell.

Alex got to his feet and tried to keep his weight off the throbbing leg. Soon the sniper was on his feet too, grinning like a shark as he removed his jacket. Alex stood between him and the gun, but his strength was fading fast.

"You should have just taken the bullet, kid," said Hansen. "It would've been a lot less painful."

Alex faced him with a ready stance, offense and defense strategies racing through his mind.

Boom! Boom! Boom!

Someone was pounding on the door to the right.

"Anyone in there?" a voice demanded.

The sniper grinned. "That'll be the cavalry," he said in a low voice, "but *my* cavalry, I'm afraid."

More voices on the outside of the door shouted to one another. "It's locked! I think he's in there."

Two more hard knocks sounded, then another voice. "Where is building security!"

"On the way, sir!" responded another.

"Get him here *now!* We need this door unlocked."

The sniper eyed the gun on the floor behind Alex. "Guess I don't need that one anymore, anyway," he said. "I've got another, and I think I'll just let them take care of you for me."

The sniper moved to the door on the right and banged hard. "Hey! Hey! It's Agent Hansen! I'm in here and the kid has my gun! Hur—"

"Hansen?" the voice on the other side said.

Alex stared in shock. *Agent?*

Hansen eased open the left door and slipped out, but not before giving Alex a wink.

Alex grabbed the door handle a fraction of a second too late. The sniper had already pulled it closed behind him.

"Shoot on sight!" Hansen yelled. "I repeat, shoot on sight!"

Alex paced the small area with his eyes locked on the right-side door. He knew they would burst in any moment. He backed away against the far wall like a cornered animal. As he moved back, the rear of his heel hit something hard. *The gun.*

Alex grabbed the pistol and raced to the left-side door. He aimed and then fired three times.

On the outside of the other door, the agents shouted even louder now. "Shots fired inside! I repeat, shots fired inside! Where the hell is building security with the key?"

"One minute away, sir!"

The bullets had torn the door's lock to pieces. Alex gripped the handle and heaved the door open. No sign of Hansen. Alex ran down the hallway as fast as he could.

There was a left turn ahead, and he raced for it, knowing the agents would be upon him any second. He imagined his back riddled with bullets.

Two long strides away from the turn, he heard them.

"Hey! Stop!"

Alex bolted around the corner and found himself in a hall lined on both sides with identical meeting rooms. A floor-to-ceiling window exposed the interior of each one. Alex picked one at random, ran inside, and gently pulled the door closed behind him.

He tried to slow his breathing as he stood against the wall, positioned so that the agents wouldn't spot him when they ran by—unless they looked back. Seconds later, five men stormed down the hall, weapons drawn.

He breathed a sigh of relief as the footsteps of the agents faded. After holding still for a few moments, he moved to the back of the meeting room and crouched behind the table that stood in the center. A deep bloodstain marred his pants, but the bleeding seemed to have stopped.

For five full minutes, Alex squatted there in absolute silence, trying to come to grips with the fact that he'd almost just died.

At last he stood and cautiously walked to the door. Through the glass, nothing was visible in the hall in either direction. He noiselessly opened the door and looked both ways.

A faint clinking noise seemed to come from the right, but he couldn't see anything. He ducked back into the room and waited; the noise was growing louder. He'd just have to retreat back into his hiding place while whoever it was passed. *Probably the agents coming back for a search.* He positioned himself behind the door, forcing himself to inhale deeply, then exhale slowly.

When he saw who it was walking down the hallway, he was overcome with joy. He reopened the door and leaned out into the hallway. "Pam! Benjamin!" he said in the loudest whisper possible.

Pam turned around first, her eyes wide with surprise. "Oh my God . . . Alex?" She lumbered toward him as fast as her secured hands would let her. Unable to hug him, she hid her face in his shoulder and allowed his arms to wrap around her.

When Alex pulled back, he looked at their handcuffs with a questioning look.

"Don't ask," Benjamin said. "Long story. Right now we have to get out of here."

"You're telling me," said Alex. "There's a bunch of agents after me, and they're going to shoot first and ask questions later. They think I'm . . . they think I've attacked one of their men, but—that's a long story, too."

"We have a friend waiting for us outside," said Pam. "She's got a car parked on the south side of the building, ready to go. We just have to get to her."

"This way." Alex pointed down the hall toward the stairwell; he knew from his and Ben's search for Pam that that's where the other door in the stairwell led. "Let's get going before they find us."

They started down the hallway, Alex leading. Pamela hadn't taken five steps before something out of the corner of her eye caught her attention. She turned to look into one of the meeting rooms as she passed.

In the open doorway stood a man.

Pamela gasped and jumped back toward the wall. Ben and Alex turned.

The sniper stepped into the hallway, slowly raising a pistol toward the three of them. "I'm sorry," he said, "but I don't think I can let you any of you leave."

CHAPTER 55

Hansen's eyes shifted from Pamela, to Benjamin, to Alex. His face betrayed his utter contempt for them.

"You shouldn't have come after me, kid."

Pam studied his every move. Moisture had formed across his hairline, despite the chilly air of the hallway. Despite the sweat, he seemed relaxed and in control as he took turns looking at each of them.

He's trying to decide who to shoot first, Pam realized.

He paused on Alex. When he spoke, his words were slow and methodical; he sounded like a funeral director. "If you're thinking about trying to lift that gun in your hand, you'd better be pretty damn fast. If not, I can guarantee that she"—he indicated Pamela with a jerk of his gun—"will be eating a bullet before your brain can get the signal to your arm."

Hansen's face changed the second he stopped speaking. He was now staring into the distance, at something over their shoulders. Pamela heard faint noises behind her. Someone was coming up behind them.

With the agent's attention momentarily off them, Pam turned her head slightly toward Alex and whispered through clenched teeth. "When I say go, shoot him."

Alex gave her a sidelong glance and mouthed, *What?*

"When I say go, *shoot him*," she repeated.

Alex gave a quick nod.

"Drop it!" the voice behind them said. "Keep coming, guys. They're all here."

"Copy. On the way," said a voice from his radio.

"Go!" Pam shouted.

She dove to her left, driving her body directly into her father. As the two of them fell to the floor, Hansen looked over, his gun following his eyes to the unexpected motion.

By the time he started to swing his gun back toward Alex, it was too late.

Two shots rang out as the bullets plowed into Hansen's chest. His eyes locked on emptiness. His gun hit the smooth, tiled floor moments before he collapsed on top of it.

Alex stood, the gun hot in his hand, unable to move.

The agent who'd momentarily distracted Hansen offered Pam a hand as she got on her feet. "You okay?" he asked.

Pamela nodded. As their eyes met, recognition washed over her. The dimpled chin, the piercing blue eyes, the Greek accent—this was the agent who'd restrained the concierge back at the Bonaventure. That day, he'd looked arrogant and menacing, a suited government puppet. Now, up close and under very different circumstances, she saw the gentleness in his eyes, and perhaps a soul hiding somewhere behind them.

He placed his gun back in his shoulder holster.

"I'm Agent Cordas. These guys were sent to pick you up," he said, "but both of you had already escaped from the cars. And I, of course, got knocked out by this guy." He lifted a disapproving eyebrow and jerked his thumb at Benjamin. "Anyway, I came to, met up with these guys on their way to the surveillance room after shots were fired. A security worker showed us a clip of one of our guys going into a room and never coming out." He paused and looked over at Hansen's lifeless body. "Then we saw this bastard leave the same room a few minutes later. We went up there and found the agent's body, along with Hansen's hideout."

Quick footsteps came from down the hall as more agents arrived at the scene. "You can put up your weapons, guys. The kid here got him."

Agent Cordas looked over at Alex. "You okay?"

"I'm fine," Alex said. "Just a little shaken—but not stirred."

The agent gave Alex a reserved smile. "Bond fan, huh?"

"Fanatic would be more like it," Pam said.

Cordas placed his hand on Alex's shoulder. "Nothing wrong with that. I'm a fan myself. In fact, Mr. Bond is probably the reason I joined these guys." He gestured at the other agents, who were busy securing each of the meeting rooms in the hallway. "You know, that was a hell of a shot. You got two rounds off before I could blink. We thought we had him back there, but you blasted your way out before we could get inside."

"Wish I'd have known," Alex said. "That could have turned out different."

The agent shrugged. "Perhaps, but you did a good job, regardless. We're all happy to have this wrapped up."

"But it's not all wrapped up," Pamela said.

Agent Cordas frowned. "You're right. We still have no idea why Agent Hansen would attempt this. Seeing how Alex here took care of our man, I don't think he'll be much of a suspect in the plot anymore. But I can guarantee you that finding who's really behind this is our top priority."

Pam, Benjamin, and Alex traded looks.

Pamela smiled. "I think we can help you out there, agent."

CHAPTER 56

President Bin had gone three weeks without a single piece of significant information. Something had gone wrong, and he had accepted that fact after the first few days. But his concern over just how bad it had gone grew steadily as time wore on. American news reports had failed to mention anything related to the sudden demise of Donald Wynn, and there was no word from his brothers or his son. Li, Zhao, and Catherine all seemed to have dropped from the face of the earth.

Bin picked up the gold-plated palace phone to check for a dial tone. He set the receiver back down on its base without dialing.

The president shifted his body in the wide chair, trying in vain to stop the stabbing pain in his hips. The week before, he had tried to prune his treasured bonsai tree. The attempt had been an utter failure; he'd stood before the tree, unable to gather the strength to lift his shears. He had retreated from the tree, two fresh branches still sprouting from its trunk.

This chair across from the television was his new home. He sat there hour after hour, day after day.

An untouched plate of food sat on the table next to him. It had replaced the one he hadn't touched the day before, which had itself replaced yet another uneaten dinner. Every waking moment was spent watching the news. Eventually some piece of information would clarify what had happened, and why. In the first day after the convention, he'd held on to hope that news of Wynn's death would break. It never happened.

President Bin's eye sockets ached from the pressure inside his head. The massive television screen blurred, and it took great effort to refocus his eyes. Just a month before, he'd been able to move through any part of the palace with ease, but that was no longer the case. He would have to lift his trembling hand and ring the tiny brass bell on the side table just to relieve himself. He now employed two attendants who were on twenty-four-hour standby should he need anything.

Outside the palace walls, no one was aware of the president's decline, but inside the staff grew more concerned as the weeks passed. They would urge him to eat and drink, but he refused almost every form of sustenance. There where whispers that his illness was due solely to a lack of food or water.

President Bin knew the real cause of his poor health. The constant waiting—the not knowing—was tearing away at his soul.

He sat up straight in his chair. A photo of his son had appeared on the screen. His aide had filed the missing-persons report the prior week, but this was the first time he'd seen the case covered by American media. He pressed the volume up as the newscaster, a blond bombshell, gave a brief overview of the case: son of President Yang Bin missing for three weeks; no leads; last seen in Washington, DC.

The report ended, revealing no new information. President Bin shoved the gold-plated phone off its stand.

The reporter continued. "And now we take you live to Wynn National Golf Course, where presidential nominee Donald Wynn is holding his second press conference this week."

The word "LIVE" appeared in the top-right corner of the screen. Several suited American men stood in a semicircle behind an outdoor podium. In the background stood a large white building and the most magnificent granite water fountain President Bin had ever seen.

After a few seconds, the man himself strode confidently to the podium.

"Thank you for coming out today," he said as cameras flashed and clicked in the audience. "I just wanted to give everybody an update on some of the progress we've been making with the current administration. I know the election isn't till November, but we're already making progress.

"You may have already heard that my staff and I worked with the current administration to implement a hundred percent tariff on all products made in China and shipped into our country. As of today, this single piece of legislation has created more American jobs in the past month than in the entire past two years combined."

The crowd exploded in cheers. Wynn leaned to the microphone. "And if you bump into President Bin and he looks pissed, I'll take the heat! You can tell him it was my idea!"

Laughter and applause broke out again, and President Bin moved to the edge of his seat. His breathing grew heavier and his knuckles went white from gripping the side of his chair.

"At the rate we're going, the deficit will be erased in two years," Wynn continued. "And with all the capital created just from the taxes we've now placed on China, you can thank them for that!"

President Bin tossed his tiny bell at the television. It tinkled to the ground a couple of feet short of its target. He placed his head in his hands as he listened to the rest of Wynn's speech.

"Sir? Sir?" came a voice in the room.

Bin pulled his head up. His aide was standing next to him, a cell phone in his hand.

"Sir, there's an American reporter on the phone. She wants to talk to you, ask you some questions."

The president motioned for his assistant to place the receiver against his face. He was now too weak to even do that.

"Hmm?" he grunted.

"President Bin?"

"Yes."

"Sir, my name is Grace Collins, and I'm from the *World News*. Do you mind if I ask you a couple of questions?"

"You may ask," said the president.

"Thank you, sir. There have been reports that you and your country are striving for world domination. Donald Wynn claimed that if he had not put the new tariffs in place, you would have attempted to control as many other countries as possible. Do you have a response to that?"

President Bin eased his body into an upright position. "No comment," he said weakly.

Silence followed his words. He lifted his heavy eyes to his aide's face. "That's all," he said, and leaned back in his chair. The young man walked out of the president's chamber as he explained into the phone that the interview was over.

Another news report came on the television as the fatigued president dozed off.

"Wynn and his camp are claiming victory for the Chinese embargo act. With the country now virtually isolated, analysts are predicting that the People's Republic of China will be forced to change its policies and work out an agreement with the United States."

"We've lost," the old man croaked as he drifted into oblivion.

CHAPTER 57

São Paulo, Brazil
November 2012

The front page of the São Paulo newspaper featured a picture of Donald Wynn and an article about the next day's presidential election. She read the article all the way through.

On the next page was another article that caught her attention. President Yang Bin of China had passed away after a long coma. The woman, sitting alone, finished reading the story, folded the newspaper, and placed it back on the table.

A steady breeze flowed across the top of the fiberglass wall outside Figueira Rubaiyat; the real glass had been replaced after the accident years before. A single fig leaf floated down from a large limb above her table and landed on her arm. She placed it in her purse for a souvenir.

She typically avoided going out in public, but this was a special day: She had just turned seventy-one. In the past, her trips to the restaurant featured limos and grand entrances, but today she waited in line like the other diners and allowed the hostess to seat her at the first available table. Amid the bustle of the lunch crowd, she went virtually unnoticed.

Life was different now. She'd once owned three homes, the smallest being a condominium in Phoenix that was well over 1,500 square feet. Now she lived far from the public eye in a small apartment in the municipality of Osasco, outside São Paulo. Her current residence was no bigger than 450 square feet.

She hadn't seen anyone she knew in months, and even if she had, no one would have recognized the woman they once knew. Her signature cropped silver hair was now much longer and dyed a deep brown. Last time she stepped onto the scale in her tiny bathroom, it showed that she'd lost forty-eight pounds. Her tailored dresses from high-end stores in New York, Beverly Hills, and Milan had been replaced with off-the-rack outfits from local merchants.

She was now Ellen Davis. The new name and her degraded lifestyle had both taken some getting used to, but she'd managed to adapt—slowly. She was even starting to think that in a few years she would grow fond of the name.

The outside seating at Figueira Rubaiyat, under the large fig tree, had always given her a sense of calm. As she sipped a black coffee in the shade, she decided she would make it an annual tradition to come here on her birthday. It would be something to look forward to in her new, simpler world.

Beyond the glass wall, she saw a black Mercedes pull up and back into a reserved spot. The owner of the restaurant, eyes covered by large sunglasses, stepped out of the car, slammed the door behind him, and walked toward the front entrance.

Okay, this is the real test now.

She and the owner went back more than fifteen years. Back then he was a waiter and his father was the owner. Both men had always treated her and the women in her club like royalty. Today she was just another customer, and it would have to remain that way.

She was positive he wouldn't recognize her, not now. She reached into her purse and pulled out a pair of wide black-rimmed glasses and slid them over her eyes. She raised the menu to cover her face as the owner stopped to exchange small talk with the host, clapping him amiably on the shoulder several times.

The owner then made his way to the patio area, moving from table to table to greet the guests and ask how their experience was so far.

She held her breath. The owner was now just two tables away. At the last moment, she picked up her ten-dollar-per-minute cell phone and pretended to talk into it. Nevertheless, the owner approached and placed a hand at the top of her back, barely touching her. "Thank you for visiting," he said softly.

Phone still held to her ear, she looked up just for a second to acknowledge him with a quick smile. Just as quickly, she lowered her head again. "What were you saying about Daniel?" she said into the phone.

The owner moved to the next table. He stopped to welcome two more tables before finally moving inside.

She released a breath. *Why even be nervous? This was Renan Santoro. He has nothing to do with anything.*

* * *

Renan walked straight from the patio to the back office of the restaurant. He picked up a bulky cordless phone and dialed a number he'd thumb-tacked to his message board. The phone rang several times before he heard a click.

He said only seven words before hanging up. "She's here. Blue shirt, brown hair, glasses."

He hung up the phone and made another call. The same seven words were repeated.

"She's here. Blue shirt, brown hair, glasses."

CHAPTER 58

T he last time she walked down this sidewalk, three years before, had
been completely different. Rather than running in a skirt, this time she
strolled casually, wearing a pair of jeans under a long brown coat. A knit
hat was pulled tightly over her head. She crossed the last intersection that
separated her from Figueira Rubaiyat. *Almost there.*

As she walked by the small clothing store, she put on a pair of large
sunglasses and swung a scarf across her face. She walked carefully; the sidewalk along Rua Haddock Lobo was just as rough as it had been years ago.

The mouthwatering smell of grilled pork floated into her nostrils; she
was just a few feet away now. The temperature was tropical—low eighties.
Sweat poured down her back; she'd worn far too many clothes for the Brazilian climate. She didn't care. She had been waiting for this moment for
years. The scent of cooking meat took her right back to the moment when
it had all happened.

The excitement made her move a little faster. When the branches of
the fig tree came into view, her heart swelled with a mixture of anxiety and
giddy anticipation. She reached into her purse and felt the cool steel of the
gun once more. It reminded her why she was there.

Everything had been arranged far in advance. As she and Renan had
agreed, the greeter looked the other way as she approached the restaurant

and let her walk inside. When she spotted the much-smaller woman with dark brown hair sitting alone at the table, she knew it was her.

Just do it. Just walk up to her and do it.

She strode directly to the table. Her right hand slipped into one of the deep pockets of her jacket. Her fingers curled around the handle of the gun. Catherine's head was still looking down, but Marisol was going to make sure she lifted it. She needed Catherine to look her in the eyes. After that, she would end it all and walk away from this nightmare. Only then would Marisol cease being afraid to sleep, afraid to dream—afraid to live.

"Don't move, stay right there!"

Catharine seemed to be paralyzed. She didn't move a muscle, didn't even blink.

Catherine finally looked up, but there was no sign of recognition.

"Just stay there and no one gets hurt!"

Three men wearing dark suits emerged from behind Marisol and moved around her. All three trained their weapons on a shocked Catherine.

"Ms. Catherine Caddaric, we have a federal warrant for your arrest."

They lifted her from her seat, but she resisted. Marisol had known she would. Once they were able to get her to stand, they handcuffed her. One agent clutched one arm, and another agent grabbed the other.

Marisol moved fast before they could lead Catherine out of the restaurant. She pulled off her dark shades, removed her hat, and then pulled the scarf from her neck. She placed her face right in front of Catherine's.

Catherine drew in a quick breath, leaned back, and tried to pull away from the agents and get away from Marisol.

Without a word, the men began leading Catherine out of the restaurant. She kept turning her head back for one more look at Marisol until she was out of the restaurant and in the backseat of an unmarked car. As the car passed by the fiberglass wall that shielded the outside seating area, Catherine stared out of the window at Marisol.

When the car was gone, Renan came up and placed his arm around Marisol.

"You all right?" he said.

She patted Renan's arm. Tears of relief flowed down her face. She felt an inner joy that she hadn't felt in years; it was the bliss of finally being free.

"I'm fine, Rene. In fact, now I'm fantastic. I . . . I've waited for this for so long."

CHAPTER 59

Dallas, Texas

"You know what, Pam? I think you need to just start working from home or something," Roxy said. "You're like a blond bloodhound with a nose for trouble."

"You might be onto something this time," Pam agreed.

Roxy spun in front of the full-length mirror, smoothing her dress around her hips. "I don't know, maybe I should've worn the red dress. This one makes me look too serious."

"Go with it, Rox. It's an election party. Serious may be the look you're going for."

Pam wandered into the living room, then stepped out onto the balcony. Closing her eyes, she allowed the cool, steady breeze to flow across her face. The scent of the city this evening was wonderful. She couldn't put her finger on what exactly it was, but it brought a smile to her face.

She opened her eyes to one of the clearest nights she had seen in years. Every star in the sky over Dallas was visible, each glinting a little brighter than usual. A nearly full moon glowed brilliantly. The occasional car passed below, but traffic was much quieter tonight than normal.

Only a handful of people occupied the streets. A woman jogged along the far sidewalk, her small dog hopping just ahead of her on a leash. On the footpath that circled the building, Pam could see the top of Mrs.

Childs's head as she shuffled toward the front entrance. Pamela grinned. The best sight of all was what she didn't see. Tonight, no one was out there watching her.

"And what are we doing out here?" Roxy asked as she joined Pamela on the balcony.

Pamela smiled. "Just enjoying the view for a sec. You ready?"

"Yeah, I guess. Didn't you say Alex was coming with us?"

Pam took another peek down. "Yep. We'll probably see him pull up, actually. Then we can just head down. These days I feel like I have to fight to spend time with him. He's built up a nice little circle of friends in Dallas now."

Roxy giggled and pinched Pam's cheek. "Aww! Pammy misses her wittle Alex."

Pam laughed along with her. "If there's anything I've gotten out of this last adventure, it was the realization that Alex can without a doubt take care of himself now. He's grown into a fantastic young man, hasn't he?"

Roxy winked. "He definitely has. And you may have had a *little* to do with that."

Pam smiled. "Why don't I make us a drink? Just keep an eye out for Alex—he's driving Dad's Jaguar."

"Sounds good to me," Roxy said.

Pam stepped inside and pulled two tumblers from a cabinet.

"How long is the election watch party supposed to last?" Roxy called from the balcony.

"I dunno—a while, but we can leave whenever," Pam shouted back. "I know my dad will be there to the wee hours of the morning, as always. I don't plan on staying that long."

"Sure," Roxy said. "Think Alex will stay late at the party?"

"Nah, I doubt it. He has to get on a flight to Spain in the morning."

"Pam, I see Alex!" Roxy shouted just as Pam was dropping the ice cubes into their vodka sodas.

Pam walked the drinks to the balcony. Ten floors below, Alex was leaning casually against the front fender of the Jaguar and talking to two men.

Roxy was still leaning over the balcony, eyes fixed on the men with Alex. Pam knew exactly what she was thinking.

"Think Alex brought a couple of dates for us?" Roxy asked.

Pamela leaned forward and looked down at the men. "I don't think either of those guys are for us."

In fact, she was positive Alex hadn't brought them dates; the dark suits immediately tagged the men as agents. God knows she had plenty of experience. On closer inspection, she caught a profile view of one of the men and recognized him as the agent who'd visited her apartment before and who was there in DC when they finally got Hansen.

Why in the world are they talking to Alex?

* * *

Pam and Roxy gulped down their drinks and made it downstairs. Alex was just coming into the lobby.

"Hey, Pam! Hey, Roxy! I was just coming up to get you ladies."

"Oh, we saw you pull up and thought we'd save ya the trip," said Roxy.

Alex gave them each a hug, then stepped back, hands on his hips. "You guys look like you're trying to catch your own politicians tonight."

Pam nudged Roxy with her elbow. "Has this one turned into a charmer or what?"

"Indeed he has," Roxy said, poking Alex playfully on the shoulder.

Alex turned and extended his elbows. "Ladies?"

They walked to Benjamin's silver Jaguar XJ, where Alex opened the rear door for Roxy, held her hand as she got inside, and closed the door. He then opened the front passenger door and did the same for Pamela.

"Everyone ready?" Alex asked once he'd dropped into the driver's seat.

"Born ready," Roxy said from the backseat.

Pam really didn't want to bring it up, but she couldn't keep it bottled inside. She decided to try the direct route.

"Alex?"

He placed the car in drive and pulled it around the curved driveway. "Uh-huh?"

"Why was the CIA talking to you?"

Alex lifted his brow in surprise. "You saw that?"

"Yeah, I did. From my balcony."

"They were just asking me a few more questions about DC," he said. "So am I gonna take the tollway south to get there?"

Pam's curiosity became concern at Alex's quick change of topic. The temptation to pry was overwhelming, but she dropped the subject. *He's a grown man now, Pamela.*

"Yeah, make a left at the light and head south," she said.

Each of them fell into their own thoughts as the car sped through the streets. Alex tapped his fingers lightly against the top of the steering wheel, keeping time with the jazz playing on the radio. In the backseat, Roxy rocked her head from side to side to the music as she texted.

Pamela leaned back into the seat and closed her eyes. There were far too many thoughts swirling in her head for her to truly rest. She thought of her dad and the company, of Formula One, and of the ordeal in DC.

Then it hit her. That's why Alex had been evasive. He couldn't tell her even if he wanted to. *I'll be damned. Is it possible that . . . ?*

Not only was it possible, it was highly likely. Alex was smart, spoke several languages, and was a world traveler. Who would be a better fit? She looked over at Alex.

The answer to the question now looming in her head was one she didn't want to hear anyway. She held her stare for a few more seconds, then turned forward.

"Hmm," she said to herself.

Five minutes later, Alex spoke without prompting. "I haven't given them an answer yet." His eyes remained fixed on the road.

Pam responded with complete confidence. "You will, and we both know what the answer will be."

CHAPTER 60

"The hell with soft power!" Ting Bin said.

The Bin brothers marched down the lengthy hall that stretched through the center of the Beijing mansion. With the passing of Yang Bin, Ting was now the oldest living brother. Thanks to the Bin family's hefty investments in China's vice president, he was now the de facto leader of the People's Republic of China. When the next election happened, the family's deep pockets would ensure their continued control of the country—almost assuredly through Ting's own appointment to the office of the president.

In the days following his brother's passing, Ting fired half of the staff that had worked under the president. Since then, the remaining staff members religiously avoided eye contact when passing Ting in the hall.

The dark mood of the staff marked the beginning of a new regime. Inside the towering walls of the mansion, Ting's reign of terror was in full effect, but it would soon reach far beyond.

Both brothers had just received the news about their nephew, Li. Feng, the younger brother, took a philosophical approach to the loss, calling it destiny's chosen course. Ting responded with anger and resentment, hanging the blame on anything and everything outside of the People's Republic of China's borders.

When Feng began to speak of the family's plans for the future, Ting shushed him and glared at the two housekeepers busy dusting the golden dragon statues that sat at the end of the hall. "In English—never in our language around others."

"They worked for our father for many years, Ting. There is no need for concern."

"Correct. They worked for our father, not for me," he said. "I trust no one. It is time to take bigger steps. We have put this war off long enough."

"War?" Feng said.

"Yes, war. No more of this soft approach. It has only been two days since we had to bury our brother, and now we find out that his only son was murdered in America. You cannot tell me you don't find that suspicious."

Feng was silent, his face unreadable.

"We both know those bastards in America had something to do with this," Ting continued. "Wynn, perhaps, or even someone he hired." Ting nodded his head, convinced of his own idea. "They'll pay, along with many others."

"It could have just been a mugger," Feng suggested. "Just like Yang. Perhaps this was the way it was intended to be. Perhaps it was Li's time."

Ting shook his head. "There is no destiny. This is something that could have been avoided. Had we taken some major steps long ago, none of this would have happened."

"We have taken those steps, Ting. We are still setting things in place, just like our ancestors did long before us, and just like Yang had planned to continue doing."

"Setting things in place and using what we have are two different issues. I urged our brother to take stronger action. Without action, no country will ever take us seriously. I'm about to change that, right now."

Feng moved closer to his brother. "It's okay, Ting. We will continue what our brother Yang started, but more aggressively now."

Ting slammed his hand into the wall. The two maids down the hall jumped in unison. "That isn't enough! Finish what he started? Our brother had been the president of China for what? Over two decades? And what did he gain? Poor health and a dead son."

Ting faced the window that overlooked a crowded Beijing street. He turned and pointed at his brother. "No, not us. This sluggish, silent war is not the way I will run the People's Republic of China. The world needs to take notice of the fastest-growing and most successful country in the world. Not later. Right now. We told them and they forgot. Now we must tell them again—in a way they will never forget."

"I understand that, Ting, but we must do it the right way. Too much attention will only cause trouble for our country."

"One cannot ignore the signs," said Ting. "When wind comes from an empty cave, it is not without reason."

The image struck Feng hard. It had been their father's favorite saying. Ting was right. Nothing happens without reason. Perhaps it was time to actively respond to the untimely death of Li and the passing of their brother.

"You always knew how to quote our father well. Even Yang often said that, of all of us, you were the most like him. I will support you. What do you suggest we do?"

"Follow me, brother," Ting replied. "I will show you."

* * *

"Are you close to a computer?" Benjamin said.

Her father's voice was so loud that Pam had to pull the phone away from her ear. She clicked the call over to speaker and motioned for Alex to lower the volume on the radio. Roxy switched off her phone to listen.

"No, we're still in the car, on the way there. You're there, right?"

Benjamin's powerful voice shot from the phone. "Hell no! I'm at the office. I'm hearing a lot of news about China."

"Yeah, us too. Seems like things have been a little crazy over there since the president died last week. Alex met him in person a while back and we were talking about—"

"No, that's not what I'm talking about. I just read that the Bin brothers are running things now, and they have decided that the US dollar is no longer the world's reserve currency. They have just sold one point eight trillion dollars in strategic oil reserves, precious metals, and Japanese yen." Benjamin paused to let this sink in for a moment. "This one move shifts the balance into emerging market currencies—the ruble, the real, the sol, the rupee, and a bunch of other Asian currencies. In other words, they're giving us the shaft."

Alex jumped in. "That's going to wreak havoc in the US and European markets!"

"Understatement of the decade, Alex," Benjamin said. "And that's not all."

Pam grimaced. "Dad, are you sure this info is reliable? Where are you getting this from?"

"This is all courtesy of your buddy Giles. He has the whole damn Internet buzzing right now. Sites are crashing left and right."

"This is horrible, Dad," said Pam. "The economy is headed down a dead-end road."

"Oh, but there's even more," Benjamin added. "The Bin brothers just had a secret meeting with the chairman of Gazprom, the CEO of Lukoil, and the president of Rosneft."

"You're kidding!" Alex shouted, his cheeks now flushed.

None of the names resonated with Pam. Roxy, surprisingly enough, did know a little about one of the companies.

"Hey!" she shouted from the backseat. "I met this guy, I think he was a chairman or something at Rosneft! Igor or something. He was in Dallas at this convention, and he kept hitting on me. Not my type at all, but offered to fly me to Moscow. I thought it was the vodka talking. Man, he could really put it away. Anyway, he kept telling me his company was worth billions—he wouldn't shut up about it. When I got home I Googled it, and he wasn't lying. It was some kind of oil company."

Alex shook his head. "They can't be doing what I think they're doing . . ."

"That dead end Pam just mentioned is more like a cliff," Benjamin said.

"I mean . . . are they really thinking about taking it that far?" Alex asked.

Silence followed. Everyone, including Roxy, sat perfectly still and waited for Benjamin's response. Pam's grasp of the situation was tenuous, but she knew this meeting had dire implications.

"Hold on, guys," said Benjamin. "I'm reading the latest cable from Giles right now."

Another long silence followed his words.

As last Benjamin released a heavy sigh. "They actually did it. I can't believe those motherfuckers actually did it!"

Alex slapped his hand against his forehead. "Oh my God! Please tell me they didn't."

"I wish I was making it up. China just convinced three major Russian oil and gas companies to cut off gas supplies to the West. In less than a week, I bet we won't recognize most of Europe. It'll look like a war zone. And you can bet your ass that the US will fall into the same hell right behind them."

Alex exhaled in frustration. "It's all over. The US has lost its influence. China now has all the power. The smaller nations will veto anything that China tells them to."

"You're damn right," Benjamin added.

Pam was beginning to appreciate the severity of the situation. "So no matter how frustrated the West becomes with China, we'll all be so intertwined that doing business the Western way will—"

"Not even be an option," Alex finished. "The whole damn world is going to have to become China's adversary to do business with them. And it's only going to get worse over time."

Pam gently placed a hand on Alex's shoulder. "Looks like you may have to return to your roots in Russia as a 'princeling' from Spain and find out what is really going on."

Alex nodded his head slowly, lost in thought.

Complete silence now filled the interior of the car. They all dwelled in the shared knowledge that the world would no longer be the same. Even Roxy understood the devastation China's actions would cause. The dark series of events that had brought the world to its knees had started long before anyone was aware of it. World leaders who had long had their heads in the sand were in for a rude awakening.

Finally Alex broke the silence, releasing the words he couldn't keep inside any longer. "I have to do something about this. And you can bet that I will use everything in my power to get to the bottom of it."

CPSIA information can be obtained
at www.ICGtesting.com
Printed in the USA
FFOW03n1343230514
5505FF